The Artist

Amorous Occupations

Cheryl Barton

Published by:
Barton Publishing, LLC

*This book is a work of fiction. Any references or similarities to
actual events, real people, living or dead, or to real places, are
intended to give the novel a sense of reality. Any similarities
in names, characters, places and incidents is entirely
coincidental.*

Barton Book Publishing
P.O. Box 962
Reisterstown, Maryland 21136
www.bartonpublishingLLC.com

Ordering Information:
Quantity sales. Special discounts are available on quantity
purchases by corporations, associations, and others. For
details, contact the publisher at the address above.
Orders by U.S. trade bookstores and wholesalers. Please
contact publisher@bartonpublishingLLC.com

ISBN:0615862780
ISBN-13:978-0615862781

Other Books by author Cheryl Barton

Bachelor Not For Sale
A Designed Affair

Published by Barton Book Publishing

Prologue

"Can you feel me, my love?" Isaac whispered in Zora's ear as she writhed uncontrollably in a sexual haze under him, relishing in the attention he was paying to her body making sure that their lovemaking experience was a pleasurable one for her.

Zora tried to form the words to respond, but the only sound she could muster up was a moan from deep within her belly as her body threatened to explode under his attentiveness to her many points of pleasure. Her mind was clouded with thoughts of floating as her body experienced flames of delightful pleasure. Her state of arousal was unmatched to anything she'd ever experienced with her husband before. Even while in the throes of desire she could sense that something was different about their intimacy. Zora wasn't complaining because as usual, her pleasure was what was most important to him and the way she was feeling and responding to him, she wouldn't trade or question the moment for anything.

"Zora, baby, did you hear me? Can you feel me?"

Isaac lifted his face from the side of her neck just in time to see her nod her head yes. He smiled when he saw how tightly she was holding her lips together attempting, as she often did, to suppress the yearning to scream out in delight. Isaac knew exactly how to get that scream he loved hearing.

Using the force behind his powerful strokes, he pushed forward and up into her body while at the same time reaching between them to stroke her hooded nub ever so gently, putting just the right amount of pressure which, as he expected, caused her to jolt under him in that uncontrollable way he loved.

"Yes, baby, I know you felt that," he groaned out trying to maintain his own composure to not lose control. He didn't want that yet because there was much more pleasure to be given. His focus was solely on giving his wife, the love of his life everything she yearned for and needed.

Isaac could feel her body building up to that point of no return as he ground his pelvis in a dance that was as old as the beginning of time. His movements brought on the delight they both savored whenever they were intimately connected.

Zora could do more than just feel that special part of her husband, but she felt him in every part of her body. His smell was intoxicating, his strong arms gave her the protection she needed to lose control and still remain closely snuggled in his embrace and the words he spoke made love to every part of her body, not just the most intimate part. The feeling of his hard flesh gliding in and out across her over sensitized love nest once again had the effect it was meant to. She tried to hold back, wanting to prolong the feeling a little longer, never wanting it to end.

"I feel you, Isaac! I love you, baby!" she shouted.

Before she had the chance to tell him more, she shattered as her orgasm slammed into her, playing her body like a drummer does a drum, in harmony. She saw what appeared to be lightning flashing across her eyelids as she held them closed tightly, allowing her body to be overtaken. She wanted more, she needed more and only Isaac could give it to her. She held on tightly, widening her legs a little more giving him even more access and an open invitation to never let up.

Zora went beyond just screaming her pleasure out, but she hollered like a wild animal in heat. She pulled Isaac closer to her, clawing at his back, pumping up as he surged in, urging him on. This was her Isaac and she wanted to stay with him like this forever.

"I never want you to forget this feeling baby,"

she heard him say into her ear, while never stopping his ministrations.

"I love you Isaac," she was able to get out and she meant it more now than ever. Even as she continued to ride out her orgasm, she could sense a change in the room. She knew they were in the bedroom of their home, their place of love and she could feel his hot, sweaty body as he made sweet love to her. There was a different tone to his voice that she couldn't get a grasp on. Even while he spoke, she could feel the pace of their lovemaking increasing as he began reaching the peak and was headed into his own earth shattering orgasm. They had been together enough times for her to know the feeling of his body craving, starving for release. She gripped his rod between her legs with each powerful thrust into her body. She wanted him to feel what she had just felt.

"Don't give up on feeling like this when I'm no longer here with you. This is more than love and you had it once with me and I need you to have it again. What you are feeling and experiencing is not meant to be a once in a lifetime feeling with one man. I will forever love you and I want and need to know that you are happy and in love again one day. Don't let this feeling die with me, so remember it so that you will want it again and again."

The moment the last words left his lips, Zora realized what was different about their encounter. Suddenly she could no longer feel the weight of his strong body pressing down into hers. She could no longer feel his soothing kisses, the ones he liked planting across her face and neck as their bodies and breathing began returning to normal. She was slowly losing her grip on his body and she seemed to be grasping nothing at all. Isaac was slipping away and she didn't know why. Her heart started pounding as she feverishly began reaching out for him, not yet opening her eyes afraid of what she might see. No longer even sensing his presence, she finally opened her eyes and sat straight up in bed feeling disoriented.

She looked around and for a moment didn't recognize her surroundings. She was no longer in the bedroom of the house she shared with Isaac, but in a different bedroom, an entirely different bed.

It took her a few seconds to realize she had been dreaming. As reality began setting in, she knew that she once again had been startled awake from that same dream she'd been having over and over for the past several months.

She took a few moments and took in her surroundings and felt a sense of sadness remembering that Isaac was no longer with her. He had not been making love to her, though it felt as real as it had years prior when they were together. Familiarity brought her back to the present and she finally realized where she was. She was actually in her house in Boston, in her bed alone.

The encounter she had dreamed about seemed so real, as real as all of the times that they had actually made love. The feelings were the same and her body reacted as it always had with him. Without thinking, she reached down in between her legs and realized dream or no dream, her body reacted as if the encounter was real when her fingers encountered a slippery wetness that proved it may have been a dream, but her orgasm was real.

Zora knew she needed to get a grip on life. The dreams were coming more and more frequent and the words Isaac spoke were a message that she still wasn't ready to deal with. Isaac, once the love of her life, was gone; he wasn't coming back and though she knew deep down the words he spoke were the exact words he would say to her if he could, she couldn't possibly do what he was asking her to in her dream. She couldn't fall in love again and no man could make her feel the way Isaac had. She knew she couldn't have him anymore, but the thought of another man loving her the way he had seem far beyond the scope of what her reality was.

Her dream and her body were clearly giving her a sign that she missed intimacy and longed for it, but she believed love like that truly only came once in a lifetime and her once in a lifetime kind of love died at the same time that Isaac had died.

She got up out of her bed and noticed it was still dark outside and she knew it was probably the middle of the night. She knew she wouldn't get back to sleep and opted instead to get up and work on one of her latest paint projects. There was no way she was going back to sleep and though she'd love to get back to her dream of a time when she and Isaac were happily married and in love, she also knew she would once again wake up to the reality that he was gone forever.

Painting always relaxed her and that was what she needed to do, after she grabbed a nice relaxing shower first. Though she felt sad, she tried to smile knowing that in the light of day, she needed to put on a smile that said happy so that no one would see that the real Zora wasn't happy; she was just dealing.

1

Zora had lots to do with little time to do it. She was more than excited about her upcoming art gallery showcase and was finally being given the chance to live out her dream of sharing her passion for art with the world. She'd experienced a lot of misery that at one time had almost become unbearable, but she'd made it through and her art had a lot to do with it.

Life had been hard transitioning from her old life in North Carolina to her new life in Boston, Massachusetts. With the hand that life had dealt her, she needed a brand new start and she was finally beginning to feel better.

Her new surroundings were enabling her to finally put the unhappiness of her past behind her, leaving it in North Carolina and now starting over fresh in a new city.

It was a beautiful sunny Saturday afternoon as

she exited her Boston brownstone smiling at the thought that life was looking up. It was a perfect day for a stroll to the local market to replenish her fruits and vegetables. On her way out, she decided to stop and check on her neighbors, the Prentiss', Ms. Sandy and her husband Mr. David, to see if she could pick anything up for them.

The Prentiss' were the nicest couple she'd ever met and getting to know them was the best medicine for a lonely soul as she was when she first arrived. They were the first to introduce themselves when she moved into the neighborhood a few years ago.

The neighborhood was in an artsy district which was just perfect for her. There was always lots to do and see and it all revolved around some type of art whether it was visual art, theater or even music. She was nothing if she wasn't all about art being an artist herself, always being interested in it even as a child. Art was how she made her living as a full-time artist and she taught art at a local school part-time combining her love for art and children. Her biggest income came from the many paintings she'd been able to sell all over the world. She'd never had an art showing like the one she was preparing for, yet she was able to still have an audience for her art via the internet and word of mouth.

Zora loved strolling through the neighborhood where she lived which was in walking distance of museums, art galleries and book stores. She didn't have that when she lived in North Carolina and she didn't realize then how much she was missing out on, being this close to any and everything art.

Her life in North Carolina was pretty much situated around the military since she lived right outside of a military base, which wasn't really close to the places she liked to visit the most. She was happy about her time spent there, but this was the best move for her following the death of her husband, who had been in the army. They were stationed in North Carolina and had been for a few years where they had settled in nicely. She happily took time for herself to focus on her painting while her husband, Isaac, spent his time in the army protecting the country.

Now, in Boston, she had come to love the Prentiss's as if they were her own parents. They reminded her of what her parents would have been like if they had not passed away years ago. Her parents had been killed when she was a young child and her grandmother, Eva, raised her, providing a loving environment full of beauty and art. She was glad that her grandmother was still alive and in great health, but she lived in Seattle, Washington, on the other side of the country. She missed home and she missed her grandmother even more.

When she graduated high school and went off to college in New York, she'd met and fallen in love with Isaac Michaels and when they decided to get married, she moved herself and her life with him to

North Carolina. He decided to transition from civilian life to a life in the military by joining the army.

Thinking of Isaac made her sad. It had been several years since he had been killed by a mortar attack while serving in Iraq. She knew she would never forget the day she opened her door to two military officers who came to bring her the news that Isaac had been in a Humvee that had been attacked. She was devastated to hear that all of the men in the vehicle were killed, including the love of her life.

Isaac was special. Growing up in Seattle, she was an outcast. She never had a lot of friends because she was so different. What made her different was her care-free attitude and her bohemian style of dress. She got her style from her parents who didn't live a very traditional lifestyle.

Her parents were artistic and were into the literary scene, preferring that over the main stream lifestyle of the day. They lived, not caring a lot about money, but more about the beauty of the world around them. They disregarded conventional standards of behavior and preferred to paint, sculpt and do just about anything with their hands.

When they died and she went to live with her grandmother, she couldn't shed what had become a way of style and dress for her and she never seemed to fit in with her surroundings. Kids were cruel and often called her names as a young girl growing up.

She was more interested in art than boys or the latest gadget like many of the kids she knew. Not much changed for her when she went off to college, though her grandmother said it would if she wanted it to. Zora wasn't sure she really wanted it to change. She was a loner, especially after the passing of her parents. Kids didn't really know how to interact with her when they found out her parents were killed in an automobile accident when she was ten years old, leaving her an orphan to be raised by her grandmother. Remembering her parents and thoughts of her grandmother gave her a feeling of nostalgia and it was times like this that made her appreciate her neighbors even more.

She gathering up her things to make her market run. As she stepped out of her brownstone, she saw that her neighbor, Ms. Sandy was on her stoop watering her flowers. Zora waved as she locked her door then headed over.

"Good morning Ms. Sandy," she cheerfully said when she reached the front of the Prentiss's brownstone.

"Hi Zora. Let me guess, you're on a market run."

"Yes I am. How did you guess?"

"Well, for starters it's Saturday around eleven in the morning and second, you are carrying your market canvas bag."

She loved that Ms. Sandy knew her well.

"I've run out of fruit and my flowers have seen better days. I was coming over to see if I could pick up anything for you."

She watched as Ms. Sandy did a quick memory check to think of any items they needed.

"I do need a few things if you don't mind picking them up. My granddaughter is coming for a visit this week and she loves fruit, especially apple slices."

"Your granddaughter is here? I thought your son and granddaughter lived in Maryland?" she asked.

"They do; well they did. My son is moving here next week and he's flying in to bring my granddaughter here so that he can get the remaining of their packing and moving done."

Zora could hear the excitement in her neighbor's voice every time she spoke about her son and granddaughter.

"I know you're happy about that."

"Yes I am. I've only seen my granddaughter in person five times since she's been born. We get to see her via computer all the time, but it's not the same. My husband and I can't wait until they get here. Listen, why don't I walk with you today? It's a beautiful day and I could use the walk. Is that okay with you?

"Sure."

"Great. Let me get my things and I'll be right back."

Zora shook her head in agreement as her neighbor disappeared into her house. She stood waiting by the fence, happy for Ms. Sandy that she'll get to see her granddaughter more often now. Once again Zora longed for her own grandmother. She'd have to make sure she gave her a call when she got back from the market. Maybe she could talk her into flying to Boston for a visit.

When her neighbor returned, they leisurely strolled to the local market. She noticed an extra pep in Ms. Sandy's step, probably due to her happiness about her upcoming visit with her granddaughter.

"So Ms. Sandy, how old is your granddaughter now?"

"She's two and a half years old and tall for her age. Every time I see her on the computer or see pictures of her, she seems to be growing like a weed. I'm thankful for computers and cell phones with cameras. Even though we don't see her often, she knows me and is excited every time she gets to talk to my husband and I. We love to hear her call us Nana and Poppy," she said with cheer.

"I can see she'll be spoiled when she gets here."

"I promised my son that we would not spoil her too much, but I'm already realizing I can't hold to that promise. I'm going to try though, but I don't know how successful I'll be."

"I'm sure it'll be fine. All children should be spoiled a little, especially by their grandparents. It's what all grandparents were made for."

"I agree. I always feel like I should give her extra, extra love since her mother passed away."

Zora could hear the hurt in her voice when she spoke of her daughter-in-law who died following the birth of the baby.

She thought back on a time, almost three years ago of how excited her neighbors were as they prepared for the birth of their first grandchild. That day started out as a great day when they received the call that the birth was getting near and they'd prepared to fly to Maryland to welcome their grandchild into the world and to be there to support their son Micah and his wife Karen after the birth. They had planned to stay a week to help out and spend a little time with their new grandbaby. They didn't know what the sex of the baby was because her son and his wife wanted to be surprised. The day didn't turn out the way they'd expected.

Zora had received the call from her neighbors that rainy day when Ms. Sandy called to ask her to pick up the mail for them for two additional weeks. She informed Zora that their daughter-in-law had suffered some complications following the birth of their granddaughter and she did not survive. Zora's heart cried for them for what they were going through. She didn't know what to say other than that she was sorry for their loss and that of course she would continue to pick up the mail until they returned. If her memory served her right, Mr. Prentiss had come home after two weeks, but Ms. Sandy had stayed an extra month to help her son with the baby. She also knew that her daughter-in-law's mother, who also lived here in Boston, had also stayed a while to help with the baby.

"Well I can't wait to meet your granddaughter. I feel like I know her already. Every time you show me a picture of her, I want to reach in to the photo and pull those thick ponytails of hers. What made your son finally decide to make the move back to Boston?"

Zora knew that Ms. Sandy had been trying to get her son to move back to Boston since the baby was born.

"It was more fate than anything else. Karen's mother and I decided to stop trying to pressure him into moving back to Boston where he and Karen were both born and raised. Did I tell you they met in middle school and were inseparable until the day she died?"

"No, I don't think you ever told me that part."

Zora definitely wanted to hear more.

"We used to be neighbors with Karen's parents since she and Micah were about thirteen years old. They were high school and college sweethearts and got married the year they both graduated from graduate school. When Micah got a job as a television broadcaster, they moved to Maryland where he now works as a producer for a major television station and Karen went to work as a newspaper reporter. After Karen died, Micah wanted to raise baby Kaia by himself and still do all of the things that he and Karen had planned to do.

They loved living in Baltimore and Micah wanted to continue with all the plans they had. It just so happens that he was offered the job of station manager for the number one television station here in Boston and he saw it as an opportunity to come back home. He realized he wanted to make it so that Kaia can be near all of her grandparents and close by where we could help him with her. His friends in Baltimore have been great helping him, but he knows there is nothing like family. Karen, like Micah was her parent's only child so Micah also wanted to get the baby back here so that they can feel connected not only to the baby, but to Karen as well. He's moving into a brownstone not far from here, so between Karen's parents and my husband and I, we'll share in the responsibility of taking care of Kaia and Micah won't have to use friends, babysitters and daycares as much as he has to now."

"I'm happy for you and you know if I can help you in any way, let me know."

"Thank you dear. You are so sweet. You are like the daughter I've never had. I loved Karen like a daughter, but they were so far away, I never got to do things with her like you and I do. Thank you for being so nice and considerate and never thinking it robbery to spend time with me."

Zora smiled. She loved Ms. Sandy and her husband as much as she could of two people who treated her like a daughter, but who were not her parents. She would do anything for them.

Once they finally reached the market, Zora went in the direction of the fresh flowers while her neighbor headed towards the fresh vegetable stands.

As she strolled, hearing about Micah and the love she knew he had for his wife, she realized how much she missed male companionship. She hadn't been involved with anyone since her husband and it wasn't due to a lack of interest from men in Boston. There were times when her body alerted her to what she was missing and now that she was comfortably settled, it was time she found more time for a social life.

2

Micah strolled through Boston Logan International Airport, pushing a sleeping Kaia in her stroller in search of their luggage. He was staying one night, but Kaia would be staying with his parents for a week until he returned after making sure the moving truck was completely loaded with all of their belongings and on the road headed to Boston.

He was thankful for the month off from work, being able to prepare for the transition to his new job as a station manager of the most popular television station in the Boston area. He was about to be the top man and had plans in mind for keeping the station at the top and drawing in even more viewers. He was happy about the move back to Boston, not just for him, but for his daughter as well. Kaia was his world and now that she was getting bigger and more aware of her surroundings, he wanted her to be able to spend more time with her grandparents.

She was the only grandchild of both sets of grandparents who both lived in Boston. It didn't escape him hearing the excitement in their voices as he told them about the new job offer that he quickly accepted. Besides the fact that he was able to move back to his home city, the salary was triple what he had been making as a producer in Maryland.

He had a few reservations about the move and the main one was that he would not be able to stop by the cemetery once a month like he does now to leave flowers on Karen's grave. That brought him sadness, but he knew in the long run, that this move would be the best for he and Kaia. While he waited for his luggage to show up, he thought about how much he missed Karen and how empty his life was sometimes without her.

He was happy and blessed that he had Kaia as a constant reminder of his wife. His baby girl looked just like her mother. She had Karen's long black hair, doe large eyes and he could already tell that she had the same sweet spirit that her mother possessed. She also had a little bit of her mother's stubborn streak when she wanted something and he would say no, she would pout and when she did, it reminded him of Karen. He had teased Karen since they were teenagers about her knack for pouting. She always denied it, but when he caught her doing it, he would point it out and they would both fall into a fit of laughter. He missed that and so many other things about her. He was still having a hard time adjusting to life without her. The only thing that made life worth living was his baby girl.

Micah looked down at Kaia sleeping peacefully. He was going to miss her for the time they would spend apart until he returned. He was thankful for his parents and Karen's parents who would be looking after Kaia until he returned.

This quick trip to Boston to drop her off would also give him a chance to see the final condition of the brownstone he had purchased for them to live in. He was lucky that as soon as he told his parents of his new job, they were able to connect him with a friend of theirs who was a realtor who had found Micah the perfect house. He had always loved the brownstones in the Boston area and knew that was exactly what he wanted for he and Kaia. He had a few things that were must haves. He wanted to be near a playground, he didn't want to be directly located on a busy street and if possible, he wanted to have an end of group unit. The realtor called him back in two days with two possibilities and from the photos, he knew which one he wanted more than the other.

On a visit earlier in the month to Boston, he did a walk through and had the realtor make the offer that same day. Once he found out he had the house, he began packing up his life and started preparing for the move. He felt like he was finally ready for a change. It was important to him to put Kaia first and he knew this move is what was best for her. It was also a good move for him as well. He would always love Karen and he knew that he would never, ever find another woman that could take Karen's place and he wasn't looking. He would be happy raising Kaia as a single parent and pouring all of his energy into her, his work and time with his family.

After getting help with his luggage, Micah retrieved the rental SUV, loaded Kaia and all the luggage in and headed for his parent's house. It felt good to be home. As he drove around the various Boston neighborhoods, the ride took him down memory lane of the days and nights he and Karen and their friends would spend riding around Boston having fun, being typical teenagers. He wouldn't connect with any of his friends on this trip because he would only be here for one day, but he knew they were just as happy about his move back to Boston as his parents were.

He and Karen's friends would often plan trips together over the years to stay connected and many would call him several times a week since Karen's death to check on him and Kaia and he appreciated that. He was back on his old stomping grounds and a little bit of the cloud he was always walking under was dissipating and he felt better than he'd felt in a long time. He had many moments where he would have a pity party because life without Karen was not what he had planned. He kept those moments to times alone because he never wanted Kaia to see or feel his anger or solemn mood when he thought about how life had turned out for them.

As he made the turn that led to his parent's house, he looked around for a parking space and found one a few doors down from their house. After parking, he went to get Kaia out of her car seat, careful not to wake her. It was early in the day when Kaia would normally have a nap and Micah didn't want to interrupt her normal pattern. After picking her up, he went to retrieve her baby bag from the floor of the back of the truck and with Kaia in one arm and the bag in the other, he turned around to shut the car door when he noticed, upon picking her up that she had dropped her favorite stuffed animal, a baby Bert of Bert and Ernie from Sesame Street, to the ground. He was just about to juggle things around to pick it up when a beautiful woman with a big, bright, lovely smile reached down, picked up baby Bert and handed it to him.

Micah was staring at her and almost forgot to thank her for her help.

"Thank you very much," he said.

"My pleasure," was all the woman said before walking off.

Micah watched her as she went up the steps next door to his parent's house and disappeared inside. He wondered who she was. He had not been home to Boston in a while and figured she must be a new neighbor since he had never seen her before. He knew his mother often spoke of a young woman who lived next door to them so perhaps that was her, not knowing which side of them his mother made reference to.

Finally making it to the house, he was about to retrieve his key when he realized he had his hands full. Just as he was about to ring the bell, the door opened and on the other side stood his mother with the biggest, brightest smile. To himself, he said, 'it's good to be home.'

"Micah!" His mother said when she saw him. She stepped back to allow him, with a sleeping Kaia in his arms, to enter.

"Hey mom."

"Look at my grandbaby. Has she been asleep long?" his mother cooed.

"She fell asleep right before we landed and has been asleep ever since."

"Take her upstairs and put her in the crib in the second bedroom. Your father had it decorated just for her. I hope you like it."

"I'm sure it's fine mom. I'll be right back. Is dad home?"

"No, I sent him on an errand. He should be back any minute. After you put Kaia down, come on into the kitchen and make sure you grab the other end of the baby monitor from the dresser in the room so that we can hear her if she wakes up."

Micah watched as his mom headed in the

direction of the kitchen while he headed up to the next level to lay Kaia down. As he turned to walk out of the room, he glanced out of the window just as the neighbor next door exited her house and walked down the street. His first thought was that she was stunningly beautiful. He hadn't dated much and hadn't even given women much thought because his life revolved around working and taking care of Kaia. He'd had many opportunities with women if he had been willing to dive it, but he had not been.

He moved closer to the window and his gazed followed her until she was almost out of sight. There was a subtle sexiness about her that made his body jump with interest. His gaze went straight to her legs, the part of a woman's body that he loved the most. The way his body was hardening and reacting to the sight of her made him chuckle as he thought of a comment from one of his friends not long ago. His buddies had been concerned that he had given up women and he convinced them that they were far from the truth. He was merely refocusing on other things that were important to him. Seeing the beauty from next door was a quick reminder not just to his eyes, but clearly to his body as well that it had been too long since he'd spent alone time with the opposite sex.

He would have to remember to ask his mother about her captivating neighbor. His immediate reaction to seeing her was new for him and now that he had encountered her and seen her, he wanted to see and know more about her.

A ringing cell phone snapped him out of his stalk-like behavior as he moved away from the window. He searched around in Kaia's bag for his phone before it woke her.

"Hello?"

"Micah, are you in Boston yet?"

He laughed hearing the voice of his friend Terry from Baltimore.

"Yeah, I'm here. What's up?"

"Nothing much. The alarm at your house went off and Candice and I went to check, but it was nothing. I wanted to let you know about it and also Candice berated me into calling to check on you and Kaia."

"We're good. She's actually sleeping and I just laid her down in the room my parents set up for her. Are you sure nothing was going on at the house?"

"Nothing that we could tell. The security firm called us and we checked everything. Doesn't look like anyone tried to break in or anything. Candice joked that it was Mariah and that she was trying to break in and unpack all of the things you'd packed up."

Micah couldn't help but laugh. Mariah was a woman that he had briefly been involved with, but there was no real chemistry so it was nothing serious. He had met Mariah while out one night with friends and things had heated up pretty quickly. He was all set for the first sexual encounter he'd have since his wife and the moment they got back to Mariah's place, there were clothes flying all over the place. He was looking forward to feeding the beast that he'd left dormant for longer than he should have.

He and Karen had a very amorous sexual relationship that started before they were married and carried over until the last month of her pregnancy. He'd gone without, out of love and respect for her, but after that night with Mariah, he was ready to get back on the horse. What started out as hot and heavy began to slow down and started to feel like the prelude to love making as opposed to a hot, steamy, noncommittal sexual encounter. He didn't want that and then Mariah spoke softly into his hear that she felt like their meeting each other was love at first sight and the encounter was then over. He wasn't looking for love and didn't want to lead her on.

"No Mariah jokes alright?" Micah said with a hint of laughter in his voice.

"Bro, I still can't believe you didn't tap that. She was more than willing and you walked away from it. I know I'm married, but I'm not dead. That woman is hot and stacked like a woman in every man's wet dream and she wants to lay all that hotness on you, buddy."

"That may be the case, but you know how I feel

about that. She's looking for a relationship and I was out to get laid. It would have turned out bad with us not wanting the same thing. I spent weeks avoiding her and when I told her I was moving to Boston, she thought I was saying it to get away from her."

"See, that's why Candace thought it was her that made the alarm go off. We figured she was trying to get a look to see if you were actually moving out."

"Bro, there's a for sale sign on my house and I'm still trying to figure out how she found out where I lived since I'd only been to her place once and she'd never been to mine. Doesn't matter now because she'll see that I am actually moving and it's not because of her. She's fine and if I was looking for something more like she is, I would have had no problem taking a dip, but now is not the time."

"Right, you have a lot going on. Well hopefully you'll find a few somethings to dip into when you get to Boston permanently in a few weeks."

"Since when did you decide to lead the committee on getting me laid?" Micah laughed.

"Hey, I'm just doing what any bro would do for another, but hey if you want to walk around with blue balls every day, you do that!" Terry exclaimed.

"Crass, Terry."

"Hey, it's what I'm known for. Make sure you kiss my goddaughter for me and holler when you get back. Let's do one last guy's night out and just maybe we can hook you up with a going away screw."

"Worry about your own sex life and leave mine alone," he quipped.

"Man, you've met my wife, so you already know that she wears me out every chance she gets and I like it!"

"It's a good thing we're friends because under any other circumstances, this would be creepy. Talk to you in a few days."

Micah hung up and without realizing it, he peeped out the window again in hopes of getting another glance at the woman from next door. He knew she was probably out of sight by now, but he hoped. Not seeing her, he checked one last time to be sure Kaia was still sleeping before leaving the room and closing the door behind him.

His thoughts again turned to the neighbor and he smiled knowing that he would definitely see her again, especially since she lived right next door to his parents.

3

Zora was glad that all of the new paints she ordered had finally come in. Some she had purchased for her class at the local elementary school where she taught part time and others she needed to complete the collection for her showcase.

She didn't want to work full-time at the school because the time she spent as an artist took up most of her time. Thankfully she was a very sought after artist whose work was prominently displayed in art galleries and homes around the country and abroad and she had several contracts for paintings that she was still working on. Her paintings had provided her with a hefty nest egg which allowed her to live a good lifestyle and also allowed her to continue painting good art and teaching a new generation to love and respect art as much as she did.

While sorting through her paints, Zora

wondered if the man she had encountered earlier on the street was her neighbor's son. She had seen pictures of him before, but she had never met him in person. She wasn't able to get a good look at him because his face was covered by the body of the little girl he had up on his shoulder.

She could tell from his profile that he was handsome. Without getting a good look at him, she could tell he exercised because the little of him that she was able to see, he was in great shape with an even greater physique. She may not be dating at the moment, but she knew a good looking, well-built man when she saw one. It had to be the son of her neighbor, she thought. It would be too much of a coincidence that a man holding a beautiful little girl a few steps from her neighbor's house wouldn't be the same man that she'd heard about. She knew Ms. Sandy was expecting her son, so all roads led to it being him she had briefly encountered.

She hadn't stuck around long after picking up the toy that had fallen and it amazed her that the brief encounter still stuck with her. She was definitely intrigued.

Running into him and thinking about him even after a brief encounter was odd for her. It wasn't as if she didn't encounter men in her everyday life that interested her. She had spent so much of her time engrossed in her work at the school and in her free time, she painted which was her escape from the world when she needed it. Rarely did she have time to even think about the opposite sex let alone spend any time with them.

With Isaac gone, she missed intimacy. She missed being in a man's arms and feeling safe and secure. Truth be told, if she were honest with herself, she would admit that what she missed most was the hard feel of a man's body against hers and the pleasure she loved deriving from it.

She missed lovemaking and all that came along with it whether it be slow and seductive or hard and penetrating like she loved. Sex was a big part of her life with Isaac and she missed those times.

She'd been on a few dates since moving to Boston, but nothing came of them. She didn't know if she was being too picky or if every man she met didn't measure up to the man her husband was. She decided to give dating a break when she realized she was spending too much time comparing them to him. She shared her dating problem with her grandmother and as the sounding board for most things in her life, she'd told Zora to relax and let life, including dating, happen naturally. She'd also given her advice to be open to change and to remember that not all men were going to be like her Isaac.

Zora hoped to find love again and if not love, perhaps she could find some really good sex and cleanse herself of the cobwebs that were beginning to form in her private areas. She still kept up her routine waxing maintenance on her private parts, but for now, they were only for her benefit. Her body was turning into a no-fly zone and that was a big change from the intimate life she'd led while married.

Her thoughts again turned to the man on the street and the deep sound of his voice when he thanked her for helping him. She didn't let it show while she was outside, but the moment she was inside of her house, she leaned back against the door and exhaled. His voice had a sexy tone to it that made her body tingle, which was something that was brand new for her. She encounters men on a daily basis, yet none had spoken so few words and had gotten her body to react in an amorous way.

As the sun started to set, Zora sat in her window seat and looked out and up at the Boston sky. This seat was her favorite place in her house to sit and gather her thoughts.

She heard conversation at her neighbor's house next door and looked to see that it was indeed her neighbor's son that she had encountered earlier when she helped him by picking up his daughter's stuffed toy that had fallen to the ground. Now she was able to get a good look at him and could see that he was just as handsome as his pictures.

He was tall, at least six feet and the broadness of his shoulders was sexy and Herculean. He was casually dressed in jeans and a pullover shirt that stretched across his taut chest. His hair was cut close on the sides and was higher on top and neatly groomed. Zora watched as he went back to the car to withdraw the luggage he must not have retrieved earlier. She watched his long legs as he strode to the car, grabbed what he needed then walked back to the house. Just before he reached the bottom step, he looked up and noticed her in the window.

After encountering him, she had left out for a few minutes to mail a letter and was glad she had returned before he made his trip out to the car or she would have missed getting a better look at him. Her heart sped up the moment he smiled and waved at her. Seeing that smile was intoxicating and had her imagining all sorts of naughty things she could do to him if given the opportunity. The man was gorgeous and not only could she see it, but her body recognized it as well when she felt the need to cross and uncross her legs to relieve a little of the pressure that had begun to form the minute he smiled at her.

What a man! she thought as she moved away from the window once he was out of sight. She needed to cool her body down and there were a few ways she could think of to do that. One involved a very cold shower and the other involved finding her paint brushes to paint to take her mind off of him. She chose the latter since painting always removed all thoughts and ideas from her mind that had nothing to do with painting.

Zora smiled at the thought of the cold shower. She'd had enough of those to last her a life time.

Micah's presence reminded her that she was a vibrant, sexual woman and now that she knew she'd soon get to see him more often, who knows what was in the cards.

**

Micah woke early so that he could have breakfast with Kaia before he left to check on his new house and then return to Maryland. His parents were up having breakfast when he came downstairs with a very wide awake Kaia. He had dressed her in one of his favorite outfits, a pink and yellow jumper. He was thankful for the wives of some of his friends who had taught him how to care for Kaia's full head of thick, long and still growing hair. He had mastered the art of ponytails and barrettes and he knew that Kaia loved it too because she'd grown fond of moving her head around until the braids clapped against her face making her laugh. She was such a beautiful little girl and he wasn't thinking that just because she was his. He placed her in the new high-chair his parents had purchased and watched as his mom got up to prepare Kaia's breakfast. Kaia was bubbly and trying to talk a mile a minute.

"Dada, dada, dada," Kaia mumbled over and over.

"Yes baby, daddy is right here. Are you ready to eat?"

Kaia bobbed her head up and down and her three fat ponytails bobbed along with her head.

"I want apple," Kaia said.

"I know baby. Nana is getting you an apple right now. You have to eat your oatmeal too."

Kaia smiled brightly at him and his heart melted every time she smiled at him. He loved her and thanked God every day for her life and he promised himself that he would never put anything before Kaia, even if it meant putting his own happiness on the side.

"Mom, it looks like you have everything covered here, so I'm going to head out. I'll call you when I get back home and I'll keep you posted if anything changes regarding my flight back next Monday. In the meantime, everything you need for Kaia is in the upstairs bedroom and of course, call me anytime, day or night if you have any questions. Karen's parents will be over later," he said.

"Okay. I talked to them yesterday before you got here. We're taking Kaia to the park today. Be careful and don't forget to call us later," his mother said as she moved about in the kitchen.

Micah's thoughts turned to the mystery woman next door. He'd thought about her after seeing her in the window the evening before. When they locked eyes, it appeared neither wanted to turn away. He broke the stare by waving and before he did something like walk next door and introduce himself, he waved and headed into the house. There was something about her that intrigued him and he knew his mother would know about her.

"Mom, who is your neighbor next door? I don't remember seeing her before."

"Oh, that's Zora and I've told you about her. She's been living there a while. She may have been out or busy when you visited before. She's over here often visiting with me so I'm sure you'll get to meet her soon."

Realization set in for him. His mother had talked about her several times.

"That's the artist you always talk about who helps you out and checks on you often?"

"Yes, that's her. Why do you ask?"

Micah didn't want to say too much.

"No reason. I saw her yesterday and curiosity set in."

He turned just in time to see his mother smile a grin that said she was already taking his question too far.

"There's nothing there Mom and I only asked because I saw her."

"You forgot to mention you think she's pretty."

Micah hated times when his mother knew him better than he knew himself.

"Yes, she's pretty. I was just asking, so don't read too much into it."

"I can introduce you if you like. I'm sure she's still home. I could call and ask her to stop over. She loves coming over here."

He knew he should have kept quiet and left while he had the chance.

"You will do no such thing. I'm already late and I don't think now is the time to play matchmaker."

Micah smiled when his mother turned and feigned innocence.

"I wasn't thinking about that at all. I've wanted you to meet her for a while now because she's a nice woman and she does look out for your father and I. Perhaps once you finally get settled here in Boston, I can have her over and you can meet her in person and I promise no matchmaking."

The thought of meeting her in person for more than just passing by as he had already done delighted him.

"Maybe."

He didn't want to feed too much into the conversation and get his mother's mind thinking of a game plan for hooking them up.

He went around to give his baby girl a big kiss and a hug.

"You be good for Nana and Poppy, Kaia, and daddy will call you later okay."

Kaia, whose mouth was filled with apple mumbled her agreement.

"Bye daddy."

"Bye Kaia. Daddy loves you."

Micah grabbed his things and went out the door. He tried to keep from looking over at Zora's house and just before he got in his car, he looked up at the window where he'd seen her the evening before and his last thought before getting in his car and taking off was that he looked forward to his move to Boston and hoped that he'd get to see Zora much sooner than later.

He reached into his pocket to grab his cell phone and realized he'd left it in the house. He quickly jogged back up the stairs into the house and within seconds was back outside just as the door to the house next door opened.

Zora was finally leaving out for work and was locking her door when she noticed her neighbor's door opened at the same time. She looked over into the handsome face of Micah. He smiled at her and her heart melted.

They both descended the stairs at the same time.

"Good morning," Micah said when Zora was closer.

"Good morning. Micah right?"

"Yes," he said as he extended his hand to shake hers.

"I'm Zora Michaels. It's nice to finally meet you. Your mom talks about you and your daughter Kaia all the time."

"My mom talks about you often when I call to check on them. Thanks for always looking out for them. She's always telling me about her neighbor who is like a daughter to them and all of the things you help them out with."

Zora blushed at his compliment.

"I care very deeply for your parents. I hear you're moving to Boston soon," Zora said.

"Yes. It was time to move back this way. I wanted Kaia to be closer to her grandparents as she's getting older."

"You have a beautiful daughter. Your mother has shown me countless pictures of her since she was first born."

"Thank you. She's definitely the light of my life."

Zora didn't know what else to say. She could stand and continue talking to him all morning, but she wasn't sure how long she could stand looking at him without blushing knowing the thoughts of him and his gorgeous body were wreaking havoc on her senses. She'd never had such an instant attraction to a man before. She needed to get to work before she said something crazy that involved inviting him over and stripping him naked.

"Well I have to get going. Welcome back to Boston. I'm sure we'll run into each other around here. It was nice finally meeting you."

Micah thought the same thing.

"It was nice meeting you too, Zora. I hope to see you again soon."

Zora turned and walked toward the metro station that would take her to work. She drove her car only as a necessity and enjoyed the daily walk to the train station since the school was only a block from her stop.

As she walked off, Micah's body was glued to his current spot and his mind was stuck on the incredibly beautiful woman that was heading in the opposite direction. Never had he found a woman as lovely since Karen.

Zora was a breath of fresh air and everything about her said life and happiness from her smile to the happy strut of her walk. He sensed it in every word she said. He watched her as she walked off in her long bright yellow, flowing dress. The lower part was free and blew in the wind while the top was form fitting and accentuated the beautiful body the dress was covering. Her skin was flawless and the beaded jewelry was perfect for her attire.

What captured him the most was her beautiful face with little makeup and the way she swooped her natural hair up into a tight bun with tiny tendrils hanging down around her head. She was so beautiful, she literally stole his breath. His mother told him of her wonderful neighbor, but she never said how beautiful she was. He needed to snap out of his trance. She was almost a full block away, yet he was still standing in the same spot staring at her. His reaction to her reminded him that he had not been with a woman since the last time he and Karen had been together. His body's reaction to her let him know just how long it had been.

Remembering he had some place to be, he turned toward his car and got in. He would definitely be interested in seeing her again.

4

Zora was in her studio working on a new painting for her art showing in a few weeks. This showing was a very personal one. She had reached deep down to discover what was in her to create for her next showing. She looked within herself and found the hurt of losing her parents, the hurt of losing her husband, the hurt of not having any children and the hurt of being different. She turned those hurts into beautiful paintings that she hoped would show people the bright spot at the end of the tunnel.

Secretly, she had been down for a long time only putting on a smile in front of others to mask the loneliness she sometimes felt. She loved how her art not only made others feel better, but they did wonders for her mood as well. She smiled admiring her work and realizing that this showing was going to be her best one yet.

The inspirations for her paintings were coming so fast, she couldn't paint fast enough to get the ideas out before they went away. She was in the midst of a portrait of Isaac that she decided to do for the showing when her cell phone rang. She looked at the screen and saw that her friend Sheila was calling.

"Hey She."

"Zora! What's going on? Did I catch you at a bad time?"

Zora put down her paint brush and decided to take a break.

"No, I was doing some painting, but I can take a break and I'm glad you called because I need one."

"Great. Guess what I'm looking at?"

Zora loved the guessing games Sheila liked to play.

"I don't know. A pink rhino crossing the highway leading four yellow ducks to safety?" Zora joked.

"Very funny, haha. Don't quit your day job to go into comedy just yet. No, I'm looking at the newspaper and I see an ad that says the Newbury Fine Arts Gallery of Boston is proud to announce the upcoming art exhibit of world renowned and local artist, Zora Michaels. Yeah, buddy!" Sheila said excitedly.

Sheila's excitement was clear and loud and she had to hold her phone away from her ear so that Sheila's loud screams wouldn't burst her ear drums.

"I'm glad the ad is out. I was told it would run

this week. I was wondering, did you also get your personal invitation?" Zora asked.

"Yes I got it," Sheila replied.

"Good. You will need it to get into the VIP section at the gallery. This showing is open to the public, but they are also setting up a special area just for those people I sent a personal invitation to. There will be some pretty big people in the art world as well as the entertainment industry in attendance from around the country and I wanted to have a special reception to welcome them and thank them for displaying and selling my art for all these years."

"Girl I'm so excited for you and you know this is major. What a great accomplishment and Barry and I are very excited for you. We can't wait for the showing."

Zora was glad to hear that Sheila and her husband Barry would be coming. She would be personally thanking them in her remarks at the showing because they have been such good, supportive friends since she moved to Boston.

"Glad to know you're coming."

"Wouldn't miss it girl. Now that you'll have this major accomplishment under your belt soon, it's time to start working on finding you a man."

Zora wondered when would Sheila stop trying to set her up with someone. She didn't know how many times she had to tell her friend she wasn't interested. She only wanted to focus on her art.

"Sheila, stop it now. I'm not looking for a man, nor do I have time for one. I want to continue to focus on my craft and not get involved with anyone."

"Zora, I hear you and you are preaching to the choir honey. You know I know your song by heart. I never met Isaac, but he seems to have been a wonderful man. He would not want you to just give up on ever finding love again and go through life without it. Barry and I have this great friend we'd like to introduce you to."

"No Sheila, not right now. Let me get through this showing and I'll think about it. I'll have some free time soon and that would be a better time."

"You always say that. Each time you give me an excuse and then something else comes up. One meeting Zora is all I'm asking for. I think you'll like him and one meet and greet won't hurt."

Zora knew Sheila was not going to give up. She had been trying for a while now to get her to meet some guy or another. She just wasn't interested, but she didn't want her friend to think she didn't appreciate her trying.

"I'll tell you what, let me get through this upcoming showcase and after everything has died down, I will do the meet and greet. After this showing, I have another project starting for a gallery in Europe for a themed showing, but I'll have a few months before I'll need to start working on those pieces."

Sheila shrieked, which made Zora jump. She laughed at how easily excitable her friend was.

"Okay and I'm going to hold you to it. Well, I'm going to let you go. I just wanted to check on you and let you know I saw the announcement in the paper. I'm glad they started the advertising early to give people a chance to plan for your big night. Bye girl."

Zora shook her head at her friend. She needed to get back to work on her latest painting, but first she needed to grab something to eat. She sometimes became so focused on her work that she missed meals. The grumbling of her stomach told her it was past time to eat.

Zora quickly clicked on the television in her kitchen as she rummaged through her fridge to pull enough together for a good afternoon snack. She was prepping all of the ingredients for a salad when the face of her neighbor's son flashed across the screen. She stopped what she was doing to hear what was going on.

It appears the number one rated television station was announcing the new station manager, Micah Prentiss. It was being reported that at the age of thirty-two, he was the youngest station manager in the history of the station.

"Wow, what a man," she said to herself. They were showing several pictures of him and each one was better than the previous. Zora had to fan herself to keep cool after witnessing all of his hotness.

"That man sure can wear a suit," she said out loud.

It appeared Micah and his daughter had settled into life in Boston and he was off and running in his new job, which according to the announcement, he was starting in another two weeks.

It had been just about two weeks since she had run into him on the street and she remembered thinking about him for the rest of that day.

Zora hoped that the transition was a good one for Micah and his daughter. She'd been so busy creating art that she hadn't ventured outdoors for more than going to work for the few hours a day. When she was focused on painting, she did little else.

She had received an invitation in the mail the other day for a reception for Micah and his daughter welcoming them to Boston. The thought of seeing him again excited her and that excitement was felt throughout her body, especially in the most intimate places. She couldn't figure out what it was that made the mere thought of him have her body heating up with a fiery desire. She may not know how to point it out exactly, but she loved the feeling it gave her.

A few times, she had seen her neighbor playing with her granddaughter in the back yard of their house. The little girl was bubbly and beautiful. Zora had seen one picture of Micah's wife and could tell the little girl looked like her mother.

She remembered how her heart sped up that day as she watched Micah walk up to them as they were playing outside. The man sure could wear a pair of jeans. They were made perfectly for him. She could see his strong, powerful, well-toned legs through the fit of his jeans and before she could stop herself, she found that her eyes had traveled further and found another imprint that appeared to also be just as impressive.

She had felt like a stalker that day, feeling guilty as she ogled him from a distance, but she couldn't help herself. Each new sighting of him was better than the one before. She remembered thinking that there should be a law against looking that scrumptious in public on the regular.

His presence brought back desires she hadn't had for a man since her husband. She thought she'd forgotten what it was like to lust after a hot man; one that was within arms-reach. She thought about her friend Sheila who was constantly encouraging her to get back out into the dating world or at the least, work on getting her some. Clearly her body was on the same wave length as Sheila's mind because they spoke the same language and right now that language was telling her it was time to indulge in the delights of a man and thankfully there was one that peaked her interest. She secretly wondered if he was seeing anyone even though she knew he had only recently moved back to Boston. A man that fine wouldn't be single for long, she thought. She looked forward to finding out and perhaps the reception for him would be her chance to find out even more about him.

**

Micah had settled in for the evening, finally finishing all of the unpacking. He and Kaia had transitioned well into their life in Boston. The house was perfect and he was glad he decided to make the move before Kaia had gotten much older and had developed relationships he would have a hard time breaking her out of.

He also knew that the transition was easier because he was back in the town where he and Karen had grown up together and where both sets of grandparents lived. He was about to put Kaia down for the night after letting her play in her high chair while he cleaned the kitchen when his mother called.

"Hi mom."

"Micah, how is everything going over there?"
"It's going good mom. I just finished the last of the unpacking. I haven't put everything away yet, but at least I'm not stumbling over boxes everywhere anymore considering it's been a few weeks since we moved in."

"That's good. Listen, did you still have things to do tomorrow where you mentioned you needed me to watch the baby?"

"Yes. Is everything okay? You have something

else to do?" he asked her.

"No, no son. I was just wondering if you could drop her off a little bit earlier. Your father and I have a few places to get around to and we want to get an early start. Rather than do it before Kaia got here, we thought we'd take her with us if that's alright with you."

"Sure mom. I'll bring her by early."

"Good and I hope you're excited about the little party we're having for you and Kaia. We're just so excited to have you home. Lila and I are keeping it real small, but if you have a few friends that you would like to add to the guest list, just let me know. Everyone can't wait to see you and meet the baby."

Micah knew that besides his mother, Karen's mother, Lila was equally excited about his move home.

"Thanks mom. It will be good to see everyone again after so long. I do have a few names for you and I'll give you those names with the contact information when I drop Kaia off in the morning."

"Okay. Oh, I wanted to let you know that I invited my neighbor, Zora. Did I tell you she's an artist and has painted some of the best paintings I've ever seen. Remind me to show you the two your father and I purchased from her that are hanging in the family room. She's also a teacher at a local school and she loves children. Did I mention that I think the world of her?"

Micah held the phone away from his ear and

looked at it as if it were a foreign object. His mother was never subtle about her intentions, but even this was beyond her usual tactics.

"Mom, tell me you are not trying to hook me up are you? Yes you mentioned several times how you feel about her."

He didn't get a response; only silence for a few seconds.

"Who said anything about hooking you up with anyone? I only said I invited my neighbor and that she's nice."

"Mom, I know you and I know what you're trying to do. If I wanted to be introduced to someone, I know how to go about it without my mother playing matchmaker."

Micah smile when he heard his mother exhale loudly on the other end knowing he'd caught her.

"Well, there is no harm in introducing you to someone I think is nice and could be good for you. I'm not saying run out and marry her tomorrow; I only wanted you to know that I invited her and, well okay, you caught me," she relented.

"I know mom," he laughed.

"I'm playing matchmaker because you seem to want to focus only on Kaia and work and I don't think that's healthy. I don't mean any harm," she relented.

"I love you mom and I know you don't mean any harm, but I've been back in Boston a hot second. Let me settle in before you start lining up potential dates at my door."

"Okay, but she's still coming to the party and I won't say anything else about it."

"No more matchmaking?" he asked, hopeful.

"I won't make that promise, but I'll try."

Micah laughed out loud knowing on the other end, his mother probably had her fingers crossed behind her back. He knew she would never give up on matchmaking.

"I'll believe it when I see it mom," he joked.

"Kiss my baby for me and we'll see you in the morning."

"Night mom."

Micah loved his mother and it felt good being close to her again. He missed her when he lived in Maryland, but he'd had his life with Karen and they were happy. Now it was good for him to be close to family and childhood friends again.

Micah picked Kaia up from her chair and could tell that she was sleepy because she immediately threw her arms around his neck, laid her head on his shoulder and before he reached her room, she was asleep. He placed her in her crib, turned on the baby monitor and went to his own room to look over some information about the station. He was looking forward to meeting all of his employees and working with them on some new ideas for some fresh, new programming. He had even received some ideas from some of the staff regarding improvements and they were good ones. He could tell he was going to be working with a great bunch of people including some of the women who had given him an eye that he recognized as interest. One rule he always had was he never played where he worked.

His thoughts suddenly turned to his mother's neighbor. Though he didn't want his mother setting him up with anyone, his interest in her neighbor was unmistakable. She was beautiful, sexy and alluring and he'd noticed those things only from their brief encounter. Since his mother was attempting to set them up, that gave him the impression that she was single which was a plus as far as he was concerned. He would hate to be this interested in someone only to find that they were already involved with someone else.

He wasn't in search of a serious relationship, but if possible, he would love to get to know her. Now that he would be permanently situated in Boston, there was a need for him to put some normalcy back into his life and that include the opposite sex. He loved Karen and he believed she wouldn't want him to stop living a full life because she was no longer here.

Micah thought back to the day he'd watched Zora walk away and remember the sway of her hips and like any other hot-blooded male, he loved the female body and would be lying if he said he wasn't interested in seeing her up close and extremely personal.

Perhaps the gather his mother was preparing for him would be the perfect opportunity for him to find out as much as he could about Zora and perhaps he could invite her out for a drink and they could talk and get to know each other. He smiled at the possibility as he settled in to go over more of his plans for work.

5

Zora had gotten up early as she often did on the weekends and decided to check with her neighbor to see if they needed anything while she was heading out to pick up a few things. She knew they were up because they were early risers like her.

Mr. Prentiss left for work most mornings before six in the morning and during the week when Mrs. Prentiss worked, she would leave at just around seven in the morning. On the weekends, they still got up early and would often sit on the deck in the back of their house and enjoy the early morning. Zora knocked on the door and waited for one of them to answer. She smiled when she saw Mrs. Prentiss' face light up.

"Zora, good morning. Come on in. I was up early baking and I need to get the brownies out of the oven. How are you this morning?"

"I'm good Ms. Sandy. You are baking early this morning."

"I know. The church is having a bazaar today and I offered to donate a heap of brownies. I've been up baking since the wee hours of the morning."

Zora could tell by the many pans of brownies already cooling that she must have started quite early.

"I don't want to hold you up. I just wanted to see if there was anything you needed. I'm headed out to pick up some things."

"Oh thanks, but Mr. Prentiss and I will be out and about today."

"Mom?"

Zora and Ms. Sandy turned at the sound of Micah coming in the house and calling out for her. Zora watched as he strode toward them and her body tingled seeing his gorgeous face. He smiled at her and her eyes darted to his perfect lips. Seeing them, she felt a tingling at the apex of her body where her thighs met. The feeling surprised her especially in the non-intimate setting of the kitchen. She needed to get her response to him in check.

As Kaia ran into the waiting arms of her grandmother, Zora watched Micah move toward her, almost in slow motion.

"Hello again, Zora."

Zora took note of the sexy way he seemed to say

her name.

"Hi Micah. Nice seeing you again."

"Oh, you two have met? I didn't realize that."

Micah and Zora both turned to his mother when they suddenly realized for a brief second, they forgot they were not alone.

Micah spoke first.

"Yes, we met when I brought Kaia to you before the move, but only briefly."

Micah was answering his mother, but turned back toward Zora unable to resist the pull to look into her piercing eyes again.

Zora hoped her reaction to him wasn't noticeable. She would hate to be caught ogling her neighbor's son while standing in the kitchen in what was a family scene with him, his mother and Kaia.

She cleared her throat, finally able to say something since she was completely overwhelmed by his presence.

"Yes we did. I was on my way to work one morning and saw him leaving and we said hello," she added.

Micah couldn't help staring at her without looking away. She had on another long flowing skirt and a beautiful scooped neck top. She was different than the nine to five suits most women wore that he worked with daily. Everything about Zora was refreshing including her attire.

His mother didn't catch the exchange between

the two of them because she was lavishing her granddaughter's face with tons of kisses.

"Well I'm glad you two met. I was planning to introduce you at the reception."

Micah looked at his mother that time when she spoke. When she mentioned Zora coming to the reception, he looked back at her. He hoped that she didn't have plans that would conflict with her coming to the reception.

"So I'll see you here this weekend?" he asked.

Zora could use a very tall glass of water. Just watching Micah speak had her stomach and other body parts doing all kinds of flip flops. Her reaction to him was crazy.

"Yes I'll be here," she replied softly, still not taking her eyes off of him, unable to look away.

She needed to get herself under control. She couldn't possibly be standing here in the middle of the kitchen in heat. She needed to get out of here before she did something stupid like ask him what kind of cologne he was wearing. Whatever it was, it was wreaking havoc on her senses. Not only was his look intoxicating, but so was his smell. She was in trouble and knew it and right now she needed some air and an exit.

"Well since you don't need me to pick up anything for you, I'm going to head out. I'll see you later Ms. Sandy."

Zora turned since she had not yet said anything to Kaia.

"You little lady are a beauty. I will see you later as well."

Kaia waved at her and Zora headed for the front door.

Micah felt anxious as he watched her leave and longed to be in her presence a little longer.

"I'll walk out with you," Micah said.

"Mom I'll be back around seven tonight. I'm going over to the station to take care of some business. If you need me before then, I have my cell on."

Zora watched as he gave his daughter a kiss then turned his attention full on her before moving toward her and the front door.

When they reached the front porch, Micah locked the door and shocked himself at how nervous he was, not knowing why. He never had a problem being in close proximity to a beautiful woman before. There was something about this woman that made him nervous.

"How have you been Zora?" he asked after they were outside and on the street.

"I've been fine. Busy with work and getting lots of painting done," she answered.

"What do you do for work?" he asked.

"I teach art part time at an elementary school. Full time, I'm a visual artist; I paint and sometimes sculpt as well. I'm currently working on some paintings for an art showcase I have coming up several weeks from now at a local gallery here in

Boston."

"That sounds exciting. Congratulations on the showcase," he added.

Zora blushed.

"Thank you and congratulations to you on the new position as station manager. I saw the announcement on the television and it appears they are very excited that you are heading things up over there."

"I'm just as excited as they are. It was time for a change and I think it's a good one."

"Well I know your parents are happy to have you back in town. I know for a fact they are ecstatic about having their grandbaby a lot closer."

"That was one of the reasons why I came back. Kaia needs to be closer to them. She's their only grandchild."

They stood as if neither had anything to do or any place to be. Neither, it appeared, was ready to leave. When no one said anything else for a few seconds, Micah decided to make his departure before he tripped up and asked her out or lean forward and brazenly kissed her. Her lips were calling out to him in the worse way and he wanted to respond by tasting them and finding a familiarity with the feel of them; something he could carry around with him all day. He immediately dismissed the thought feeling like a crazed man.

"Well it was great seeing you again Zora. You look beautiful."

Micah's compliment caught her off guard. She stammered out her thank you.

"Thank you and if I don't see you again soon, I'll see you at the reception," she said.

In a repeat of the first time they'd held a conversation on the very same spot, she turned and walked in one direction as Micah headed toward his car.

She held her breath until she knew she was out of his sight and then paused to slow down her speeding heart. She felt like a teenage girl with a crush on the most popular guy at school. Her pulse was racing and if there had not been a slight breeze out, she would be sweating right now. What was wrong with her? She had met plenty men before and after Issac, but she had never had a reaction to any like her reaction to Micah. She was in trouble.

**

Micah sat in his car for a few moments to gather himself. He wasn't sure he would survive continued interactions with Zora. He felt like a young boy who wanted to draw a note that said 'would you like to go out with me' with a place for her to check yes or no. He now knew that his instant attraction to her the first time they met was not a fluke. It happened again, and this time it was more powerful.

He felt more comfortable around her. His body had the same reaction though each encounter was more intense. He could feel certain parts of his anatomy rise as if a signal had been sent out that he was about to get some action. He took a moment as he did the first time he'd met her and adjusted his growing manhood. It seemed to find her attractive as well.

"Down boy," he said talking to his penis which seemed to have a mind of its own around Zora. Another reminder that being around her was giving his vow of no women until he got his life back on track a run for its money. Finally adjusted and in a more comfortable position, he was about to pull off when the vibration of his cell phone made him jump. He shook his head at himself while reaching for his phone and deduced that he needed to get his mind and his body in check.

"Jake, man what's going on?" he asked the minute he saw the Baltimore phone number appear.

"Not much on this end. I'm checking to see what's happening on your end. How is the move coming along?"

"Still trying to get settled though Kaia is settling in quite nicely. Her grandparents are keeping her busy and she loves being around them."

"Glad to hear she's settling in good, but what about you man? I know moving wasn't an easy choice for you."

Jake was right. Even though Boston is his home town, he still felt like a stranger to the area, but assumed things would change with time.

"I'm good. It's odd being back here, but I'm

looking forward to the change though I'll miss everyone in Baltimore. What are the guys getting into tonight?" he asked.

"You know one of our usual spots except for the fellas on lockdown by wives. There is no hope for them," Jake laughed.

Micah laughed out loud along with him. That was a joke amongst he and his friends. His married friends had to play cloak and dagger exercises to get out for an evening where as he and the other single guys were free to go out and do whatever they chose without worry about repercussions when they got back home especially if they returned home smelling like alcohol and perfume.

Micah didn't have that problem with his wife in the past because Karen trusted him and knew that he needed the outlet with his friends.

"What's the spot of choice tonight and are there women involved?"

"No, nothing like the wildness you know we are prone to get involved in. There is a black tie professional mix and mingle event tonight and we plan to hit that up and possibly hit up a ladies night out spot afterward to really unwind. Terry is hanging out with me though I'm surprised Candace is letting him out. You know she only trusts you to keep Terry in line when he's with the fellas. She thinks the rest of us will let him fool around and lie for him, something she knew you would never do. Speaking of ladies, I hope you plan to lighten up and go out on a few dates, meet some women once you're settled in. You know it's time and as much as you know I love Kaia, don't use her as an excuse to not get out and live again."

"You sound exactly like Terry. He gave me the same speech recently. Did you guys rehearse this together?" he quipped.

"Funny dude. We're all just worried about you and want to be sure you're getting back on the horse."

Micah appreciated everyone's concern.

"I'm always going to live, you know that. It's been crazy when I think of all the plans Karen and I had for our lives, having more children and traveling. There are days where it's still hard to believe she's gone and so I've had to dive in to make up for her absence with Kaia. I don't know if I'm ready to add a woman to that equation."

Micah said that even while thinking about Zora, someone he had a feeling could make him change his mind.

"Micah, who said anything about adding a woman to your life with Kaia. I'm talking about getting out, having some fun and getting you some."

"Yeah, well I'm sure you're getting enough for us both. Twins Jake? You know I heard about the twins you hooked up with. Seriously, sisters?"

Jake breathed heavily on the other end.

"Micah all I'm going to say is don't knock it until you try it. It was wild, dirty, nasty, kinky and any other porn-like words you can come up with."

"Dude, too much information," Micah jibed.

"Right, I'm just saying, life is too short to be all about work and no play. I know there are some fine women in Boston. Next time I call I want to hear some stories about panties flying across the room and you indulging in as much nakedness as you can stand. It's part of the bro code that you do that, especially as a single guy," Jake snorted.

"I almost forgot you have no filter at all, bro," Micah added.

"Hey, take me as I am!" Jake hollered.

"There are plenty of lovely women here in Boston and in fact I met one who happens to live right next door to my parents. You know me, I don't speak about instant attraction, but this woman and her beauty are haunting me."

"Have you asked her out yet?"

"Jake, I haven't been here that long. I only said she was beautiful and she is. You are worse than my mother who is already trying to hook me up with her."

"See, even your mom thinks it's time for you to get back on the horse."

"Well, I'm good if everyone leaves my love life to me. As a grown ass man, I think I can figure it out pretty well on my own."

"Please, dude, ain't nobody talking about love. Maybe your mom is, but I'm talking about headboard banging, hot, raw, nasty, dirty, porn star kind of sex."

Micah couldn't control his laughter at this point. Leave it to one of his best friends to keep things honest."

"Right, headboard banging, got it. I need to get going. Tell the gang I said hey and I'll be back that way soon."

"Hopefully with some stories to tell about all the sexy women in Boston. You have to let me know what I'm in store for when I come to visit. Being one of the last few in our group that's not married, I'm getting it all in."

"Later Jake," he said before hanging up.

Micah looked back down the street, knowing he wouldn't see Zora, but his thoughts turned back to her. For the first time in a long time, he was ready to get back into the dating arena and he was hoping to do it with the artist next door.

6

Micah knew the moment Zora had entered the house. He could sense her presence as if they were already connected on an intimate level. He looked up from talking to a few of his childhood friends and spotted her as she entered the living room of his parents' home. He was drawn to her especially after seeing how exquisite she looked and he was no longer interested in the conversation he was having. He excused himself and went to say hello.

Micah kept his eyes planted firmly on Zora as he made his way through the crowd of people who were milling about. He shook his head at what his mother called a small gathering of what seemed to be at least a group of sixty or so. There were people everywhere, but all he could see and focus on was Zora. He was happy to be able to see and hopefully converse with her in a relaxed setting. Though he was excited to see everyone, his day was spent with thoughts of seeing Zora again.

When he finally reached her, there was something in the way she looked at him that said she was just as interested in him as he was in her. They smiled a friendly smile filled with knowing and excitement and at that moment it seemed as if there was no one else in the room except the two of them. The sizzle between them that continued to be around when they encountered each other had once again returned. The unspoken attraction was louder than all the conversations in the room put together.

"Hello Zora," he said the moment he was close enough for her to hear him.

Zora shivered when the sexy, deep, baritone sound of his voice sent her body on high alert.

"Hello Micah."

"I'm glad you made it over."

"I wouldn't miss it."

Zora did a quick scan of his attire.

"You look very nice tonight, Micah."

"Thank you. You look lovely tonight, but then again, every time I see you, your beauty seems to steal my breath."

Zora stepped out on faith and didn't hold back on her comment. She knew that he wasn't the only one who had trouble breathing when they were around each other.

"I understand," she whispered, never taking her eyes off of his. Without thinking, she let her eyes leave his and looked down at his lips and before her brain could register a thought, her body was already tingling with the thought of all the ways she would love to feel those lips.

"Do you?" he asked without a hint of reservation. It looks like they were going to be honest with each other in a room full of people and Micah was more than ready. His plan to take it slow and ease her into her interest in her went out the door the minute he captured her eyes.

Looking penetratingly back up and into his eyes she said, "Yes I do and believe me the feeling is mutual."

Zora's palms felt sweaty and though she should be nervous with where the conversation was definitely leading, she didn't want to stop until it was crystal clear that they were on the same page.

They stood in silence never taking their eyes off of each other. Micah leaned forward and spoke closely next to her ear because he wanted to be sure that no one standing nearby would be able to hear him.

"I don't make it a habit of being too forward, but I want to be sure you understand what I'm thinking. I think you are one gorgeous woman and if we were not in a room full of people right now, I would show you the effect you have on me every time I see you. Perhaps you'll give me the chance to do that, if I'm not being too forward here."

Zora was glad he said something because in all

of her preparations for the party, she had talked herself into telling him that she more than enjoyed talking to him and that she hoped the interest she thought she saw on his face when they spoke was in fact an interest in her. Gone is the day that women no longer spoke their minds when it came to wanting a man and she was more than ready to let her want for him lead her.

She was so overwhelmed by his boldness that she was afraid to speak knowing that she wanted to reply that she'd love to leave the party and let him show her before she lost her nerve. Instead, she nodded her head and smiled, letting him know his thoughts mirrored hers.

When he leaned back and she was once again able to look him in the eye, she was sure there was no mistake in the message she was giving back to him. Neither said another word, but let their glances at each other speak for them.

The moment was broken when Micah's mother walked up to them.

"Zora, so glad you could make it. You look very nice. She looks nice doesn't she Micah?" his mother asked not looking up at him, but continuing to smile at a now blushing Zora.

Micah who had never taken his eyes off of Zora agreed.

"Yes she does and I was just telling her that."

Zora didn't let the moment pass her by without adding in a compliment of her own.

"I was also telling Micah that he seems to get even more handsome every time I see him."

The jubilant look on his mother's face was something Micah didn't have to see to know was there. This was her plan all along.

"I knew this party would be a great idea and a time for two of my favorite people to meet, though I hadn't known you had actually met before I decided to plan this."

Zora turned to her.

"Thank you again for inviting me."

"I can't tell you how glad I am that you came. Micah, Kaia is ready for bed. I put her pajamas on so you just have to put her in bed. Your dad and I will keep her tonight. Why don't you pick her up tomorrow. Perhaps the two of you would like to go out after the party. Boston has changed a lot Micah and I'm sure Zora would love to point out some new sights and places you young people hang out at."

He looked at his mother mystified at her boldness.

"Really, could you be any more obvious her mom?"

They all smiled as Micah took a very sleepy Kaia from her arms. When he did so, Kaia rubbed her eyes and looked over at Zora. When she saw her, Kaia said, "Pretty daddy."

He knew she was talking about Zora.

"Yes baby. She is very pretty."

"Kaia pretty too daddy?"

"Kaia is very pretty and sleepy. Zora excuse me while I put her down. Mom, move away from Zora and go visit with some of the other guests before you embarrass her to the point that she'll want to leave before I get back."

When Zora laughed, his mother punched him lightly on the shoulder as she walked away, smiling and shaking her head.

Micah caught Zora's gaze before he moved.

"Don't leave before I get back. I want to speak to you again before the end of the night."

"I'm not going anywhere. I'll be here when you get back," she eagerly admitted.

Micah smiled his understanding as he headed to the stairs, knowing that tonight was the beginning of something fresh and he was ready to see where things were headed.

Zora watched Micah until she could no longer see him on the stairs. When she turned around, she encountered a very happy Ms. Sandy who had quickly returned to her side.

"Am I obvious about my desire to introduce you to my son? I hope I'm not putting either of you on the spot. You know I love my son and knowing him and knowing you, I felt that if nothing else, you two could become friends."

Zora knew better than that.

"Ms. Sandy, I know you better than that and you knew that if we met, there would be an instant attraction and you wanted to be sure neither of us ignored it."

Ms. Sandy smiled sheepishly and Zora laughed.

"So I wasn't being nonchalant about my intentions?"

"Not even a little bit and it's okay."

"I'll leave it alone and get back to my guest. Make sure you get something to eat and mingle about."

Zora turned to spend some time mingling with other guests at the party waiting for Micah to return.

**

The reception was winding down and everyone seemed to have had a great time. Micah was helping his mother and Zora put the kitchen back in order while his father went to check on Kaia.

The party had turned out to be a good idea. He got the chance to see a lot of family he had not seen in a long time and he was able to catch up with a lot of childhood friends, but best of all, he had a chance to spend some time really getting to know Zora.

After making his rounds at the party making sure he greeted each person, he once again sought out Zora and found a quiet spot where they were able to sit and talk.

He listened while she told him all about the kids she taught art to and how much enjoyment she got out of two her of her favorite things combined into one; kids and art.

When she mentioned to him days before that she

was an artist, he googled her one evening and discovered she wasn't just some small time artist. She was well known around the country and outside of the country as well. She had made a small fortune selling her paintings and doing art shows around the country for years. He was really impressed when he saw some of her pieces and knew why her art was so popular. She had great talent.

In talking to her tonight, he had found that her favorite color was blue, her dad was of bohemian descent and she had continued with the lifestyle her parents lived when she was a child. She didn't have anything against mainstream life, but she preferred a quiet existence that consisted of her and her paint brushes.

She had been married and like him, had lost her mate. It broke his heart to know the circumstance by which her husband died, but he was thankful for the service he provided in protecting the citizens of this country.

Her favorite musical artist was Marvin Gaye and her favorite movie was The Wiz, starring Diana Ross and Michael Jackson. Her favorite author was Zora Neal Hurston and they both laughed realizing it would be a waste for her to be named after the woman and then not love her craft. She loved going to museums, aquariums and zoos and she loved nature and all of the things in it. He loved talking to her and his body loved being around her. As much as he tried, he could not stop his body's reaction every time he came close to her. He feared someone would notice his constant state of arousal every time she was near him. He guessed that's what happens when you haven't been intimate with a woman in almost three years.

Zora was finally finished putting the dishes away after washing them. She watched Micah as he talked with his dad about work stuff and about his first full work week at the station.

She thought back over the evening, not doing much socializing with everyone, but most of her time was spent talking to Micah. She couldn't seem to get enough of being around him. Once they started talking, they forgot others were in attendance. Micah took the time to greet all of his guests, but he always found his way back to her to continue their conversation. She had discovered much more about him than the few bits of information she had learned from his mother.

She of course knew that he had lost his wife who died right after giving birth to their daughter, from a brain aneurism. They think that she'd had it for a while and it burst during the stress of giving birth. It broke her heart knowing what he must have gone through and she remembered the hurt and loss his parents had gone through.

She discovered that Micah loved science fiction movies most of all and that he proudly proclaimed himself a Trekkie due to his love of all things Star

Trek.

His favorite food was any type of breakfast food which he loved eating any time of the day or night. He'd always wanted children and had wished he'd had a chance to have more children than just the one he had, but fate did not play him a fair hand. He wasn't depressed about it and was thankful for his little girl.

He, like her, had gotten so wrapped up in focusing on work since the passing of his wife that outside of taking care of his daughter and working, he didn't do much else. He loved music of all kinds and his favorite performer was Jay-Z. She felt bad that she monopolized his time, but he didn't seem to mind and neither did anyone else. They had talked about taking in a movie or going someplace to get something to eat one night and she looked forward to doing that. It was getting late so Zora started gathering up her things to head next door to her own home.

"Thank you for the invitation tonight. I had a wonderful time," she said as she spoke to Micah and his parents.

"We're glad you came dear."

Micah didn't want to lose the opportunity to be with her a little longer.

"Zora, wait, let me walk you out. Mom, dad, I'll see you both in the morning when I pick up Kaia. Thanks for keeping her tonight and I'm glad I don't have to break her sleep to get her home."

After making sure everything was locked up, Micah escorted Zora out of the door and over to her door. When they walked up her steps, they stopped and faced each other.

"Thank you for walking me next door. You really didn't have to, but I appreciate it."

He didn't respond. All he could think about was the kiss he wanted from her delectable lips since she'd arrived at the party. His desire for her wouldn't let him wait any longer. With her standing on the step above him, which put her mouth level with his. He looked from her eyes to her lips and then back up to her eyes again as he slowly moved closer and closer to her. He knew he wanted to kiss her, but he moved slow giving her the chance to step back if she didn't want him to.

As he came closer and closer and as his breath quickened, he waited for a sign to stop from Zora and when he saw none, without missing a beat and making it seem like it was the most natural action in the world, Micah leaned forward, pulled Zora closer to him and before she could think about what was about to happen, he kissed her. He didn't just kiss her lightly on the lips, he devoured her lips leaving no doubt that he'd been thinking about the kiss all evening and now given the chance, he was putting his all into it.

Zora was swept up in a moment that she never wanted to remove herself from. The deep, ardent kiss had her feeling all tingly inside. She hadn't felt this way in a long time as she leaned into the kiss to let him know that she was enjoying it just as much as he was. She sought out his lips and reached up to brace herself by holding on to his shoulders as he proceeded to deepen the kiss even more by going after her tongue. He lapped at her trying to get more and more of her. She made sure she didn't make it hard for him to do so by willingly opening up to him. Foreign to her, the floodgates of raw emotion opened as she relaxed and joined in the kiss that sent an intense feeling from her breasts to the area between her legs. All she could think about was how good he was making her feel and how good things would be between them if they were closer to a bed.

A jolt as strong as lightening shot through Micah. He had never experienced such raw passion from a kiss before. The experience was equal to a thirsty man roaming through the dessert until he encountered a stream of cold, flowing water.

The very second his tongue tasted hers, he was lost and it was becoming his undoing. He knew he needed to pull back because anyone walking by would encourage them to get a room since he was standing on the step making love to her mouth like a starving man.

As his body hardened from the magnitude of the fiery kiss and their close proximity, Micah was drawn to pull her even closer, allowing her to feel how much he wanted and desired her. He

71

continued to stroke the inside of her mouth as her arms reached up and pulled him even further into her space, leaving no room for air to seep in between them.

The kiss seemed to go on forever and Zora felt like she would never get enough of kissing him. He was pulling feelings out of her that she had not felt in years. She knew her attraction to him was like a live wire, zapping with electricity. She had no idea it would be as powerful as it was.

When Micah finally broke the kiss, they were breathing hard to the point that neither could speak. The shock of the encountered resonated on their faces as neither could pry their eyes from the other. It was apparent neither had been prepared for the impact. Zora smiled at the thought that to a stranger, they were acting like two horny teenagers. When she could muster up a few words, she knew what the next step was. There was no way she was letting him leave yet. She needed to experience more of his kisses, but standing in front of her door within eye range of his parents was not the place to do it.

"Would you like to come in?"

Micah didn't wait even a breath after the last word left her mouth.

"Yes."

7

Zora was breathing as if she'd run a marathon. Her excitement was on a level she'd never experienced before. Micah was inside of her house and there was no turning back now. She knew she needed more than the sample kiss he'd given her outside. That kiss had set off a fire in her that only more of his kisses could extinguish.

Once Micah had passed by her with a look on his face that said he had an agenda, she turned and locked the door ready for him and whatever he had in mind.

She turned back around to follow him into the room and walked right into a wall of chest; his chest, the one she'd had dreams of touching, kissing and licking until they both screamed through their haze of longing for one another. The minute she encountered him, she realized he had not moved.

She looked up into the deepest, darkest, blackest eyes she'd ever seen and became lost in the bottomless pools. They were glazed over with a craving for her that gave her pause. She wanted this man more than she wanted to breathe.

Moving at the same time, they reached for each other and suddenly arms and lips were flying everywhere. Neither could contain the ache or the pain of desire that was enveloping them. It was an ache that they knew could only be satisfied when they were naked and screaming each other's names. Clothes were coming off with the speed of light while neither took note that they were still standing in the foyer that led to her living room and the stairs to the next level.

Micah watched as Zora looked from him to the stairs as they continued stripping each other of every article of clothing. He knew what she was thinking, but he wasn't sure he'd survive a trip up the steps to a bed. He wanted her and he wanted her now.

"Zora, I really would like to take this to a bed someplace, but I don't think I can wait. I need to be inside of you right now. I don't know what's happening to me, but my need for you can't wait much longer," he crooned, shivering at the sound of desperation he heard in his own voice.

Zora didn't respond, but her eyes followed the trail of his hands as he reached down to remove his boxers, the last article of clothing he was wearing.

Seeing how ready he was for her, she knew she didn't want him to wait either. He was long and thick and her mind was already imagining how good he would feel once he connected their bodies in the most intimate way possible. More than anything, she needed to feel him. It had been a long time for her and the thought that this man wanted her as much as she wanted him convinced her that she didn't want to wait either.

She reached out and grabbed his long, stiff member and stroked him lightly at first before increasing the intensity, enjoying the look of extreme enjoyment on his face as he tried to hold back from giving in to her touch.

Micah stopped breathing. He didn't know what else to do once Zora had reached out and began stroking him as he begun to lose all train of thought. All he could do was feel and feel is what he did.

He closed his eyes and held his head back only concentrating on how good her small, soft hands felt on his heated, sensitive manhood. Though her hands were only stroking his member, he could feel her touch throughout his body and the embers of lust continued to grow as she stroked him harder and faster while at the same time leaning forward to place kisses across his bare chest. His body began moving on its own as he began thrusting and pumping his hips back and forth, in and out of her grip.

"Zora, you're killing me baby," Micah groaned while trying to reign in on the feeling to race to a release. He needed a distraction so that what was happening between them wouldn't be over before it got started.

He leaned down and captured her lips in a passionate kissed filled with everything he desired and couldn't wait to show her. He used his tongue to part her waiting lips and dived in going in search of her tongue, dueling with it for control. He loved that she gave as much as she was receiving and before long, they were both panting unable to control the need to get as close as they could.

As he deepened the kiss, he drew Zora closer to his body as her arms ran up his chest to encircle his neck bringing him down even harder on her mouth. He couldn't resist reaching up and grasping her breasts into his strong hands, immediately stroking the tips until they pebbled hard and strong under his caress. When Zora moaned into his mouth he cupped her breasts, rolling the nipples between his fingers while giving the nipples a light squeeze.

"You feel incredible," he whispered once he released her lips, momentarily to breathe before going back in again for another prolonged taste. He delighted knowing that Zora felt and tasted like everything he thought she would from the moment he'd met her.

Zora luxuriated in the kiss as she tried desperately to hold on to his shoulders to avoid collapsing to the floor when she began feeling lightheaded. She felt the kiss from her head to her toes as she curled and uncurled them.

"I really hope I'm not dreaming and that I don't find myself waking wake up to find that this isn't really happening, but that I'm having another dream about you," Zora admitted.

Micah pulled back and looked her in the eyes.

"You've been dreaming about me?" he asked, excitedly.

Realizing it was too late to take back her admission, she nodded her head not feeling the least bit ashamed.

Not wanting to lose their close connection, she placed soft kisses across his chest as she explained with one word at a time between each kiss she planted.

"I've had several dreams about you and though they were exciting and as erotic as one could get in a dream, nothing compares to having you right here, in my house naked, aroused and oh so ready and so am I."

To prove her point, she reached back down and grabbed his hardened flesh in her palms realizing his size prevented her from getting her hand all the way around him. She softly and slowly caressed him again letting him know that he wasn't the only one ready.

"I must admit that I too have had a few wet dreams about you as if I were a fifteen year old school boy again, but the real thing more than makes up for the nights when I wasn't close to you like this. Now, no more talking because in my opinion, we've waited long enough."

Zora placed one last kiss on his chest.

"You had me ready for you at the first hello."

She then took his other nipple between her teeth and he almost growled. She loved the way he was responding to her touches, caresses and kisses.

Micah knew he wasn't going to last much longer. He reached down to pull her lips back up to his. He needed to slow things down a bit. After taking her lips in another explosive kiss that he hoped made her toes curl like his, he lowered his head to her chest so that he could caress her breasts with his tongue.

As he sucked her into his mouth and heard her gasps of delight, he thought back to the moment when she'd removed her bra and her mounds came out to greet him. They were as large and luscious as he imagined they would be. Not only were they big, which heightened his arousal even more because he was a breast man, but right before his eyes, they pebbled to hard points, standing firm at attention waiting for him.

He kissed around the outside of the globes before setting his attention on the chocolate, pointed tips. He sucked and caressed them with his tongue as he relished in hearing Zora moan out her satisfaction.

While he lavished attention there, he reached down to remove the last piece of clothing that came between them; her very tiny, barely there black panties. He needed to get closer to that part of her that was calling out to him. He released her nipple long enough to pull them down her long, shapely legs. When he had them removed, he looked his fill and basked in the glow of her beauty. Seeing her bare before him, his yearning for her multiplied ten-fold.

"Zora, I would love to find a bed and make love to you slowly, but this first time is not going to be like that. I feel like I'm struggling to hold back and I can't anymore; I need you."

Zora knew how Micah felt because she was barely holding on herself. She was so overwhelmed with emotion that she nodded her approval to whatever he wanted to do.

She watched as he fumbled in his pants pocket in search of a condom and with shaky hands, she watched as he ripped one of three condoms from his wallet and tried to tear it open. Zora could see that he was just as anxious as she was and decided to help him along knowing she needed him as badly as he needed her.

"Let me," she said, taking the condom from him. She opened the wrapper, removed what she knew was a magnum sized condom and proceeded to roll it on his bulging flesh.

Micah watched Zora place the condom on him

and he gritted his teeth as she did so. Her hands on him was almost too much to handle. Just being around her had his body craving for release, but now to have her touch him like this, his yearning had turned to a hunger.

Micah reached for her, lifting her off of her feet and moving until her back was against the closest wall. When he was sure she was firmly against it, he kissed her again, letting her feel his want as he slowly moved his hips and his arousal against her while his kiss fed his and her want and need for each other. He broke off the kiss long enough to brace his legs so that he could hold her up right before wrapping her legs around his waist and as he looked deep into her eyes, he entered her body slowly and methodically making sure they both enjoyed his entrance into her. Micah stopped briefly taken back by the glorious feel of her body encasing him like a glove. He wanted to push in to the hilt on his first pass, but he took his time. It was the only time he would go this slowly because once her body was acclimated to his entry and his size, he was going to love all over her like it was going to be his last time.

Zora exhaled on his first attempt at entry into her body. She gasped in pleasure and also at the sheer magnitude of his large member. Briefly her mind questioned if he'd fit, but what started out as a slight touch of pain turned into the most incredible feeling in the world.

As the liquid essence flowed from her body coating her and him, proving how turned-on she was, his passage in and out of her body became smoother and easier. Zora sighed on his final push all the way into her body and she joined in the slow movement as her hips begin grinding to match his movement. He was deeply seated all the way and as she closed her eyes, she saw stars.

"You feel incredible Zora, absolutely incredible," Micah said breathlessly as he pushed in and out of her body over and over again.

Zora added to the pleasure by riding up and down on him using the wall behind her as a brace. She tilted her head to receive the kiss she saw coming and held on tight to his shoulders to not slip out of his embrace.

"This feels so good," she whispered in his ear. "I knew it would be this good with you," she said as she continued to ride him, feeling every plunge of him into her body, from her head to her toes. When Micah quickened the pace and whispered her name over and over in her ear, all semblance of restraint went out the door as an orgasm slammed into her taking her heights she'd never experienced before. Tantalizing sensation after tantalizing sensation shot through her as she rode through the storm, trying to stymie her screams by biting her lip, but the overwhelming pleasure took over and she moaned then screamed out loud releasing her desire.

Micah knew the end was coming as he exploded, screaming out her name the moment he heard Zora let go. He held on to her, not wanting to drop her as his legs became weak from the potent release that had him growling like an animal in heat. He couldn't control the feeling and the sounds he was eliciting even if he tried. He closed his eyes, leaned into her neck and muffled out his pleasure as stars formed behind his eyelids.

They were both lost in the euphoric feeling while the only sound that could now be heard in the room was their breathing.

Micah stood on shaky legs, holding Zora in place not wanting to break their intimate connection. He loved the feeling of having her in his arms and being connected to her sexually. Using the little strength he had, he leaned back and without speaking, he placed soft kisses all over her face. He felt her shutter and wondered if she was uncomfortable. He lifted her so that he could extract himself from her body without putting her down on the floor. He looked around, remembering he never did get a tour of her house so he didn't know where anything was.

Zora saw Micah looking around after lifting her further in his arms and knowing his intent to find more comfortable spot, she pointed to her living room. As he turned in the direction she'd pointed out to him, she wrapped her legs tightly around his back as her arms once again encircled his neck. She didn't know what to say or what would happen with them next, but she did know she didn't want the night to end.

**

It was early morning when Zora finally woke up from her brief nap after two more rounds of unbelievable, out of this world, toe curling sex with Micah. First in her living room against the wall and then in her bed where they finally made their way to after kissing and caressing on her sofa. When they realized they had once again awakened the sexual beast in them, Micah lifted her and carried her up to her bedroom. For her, this was years of pent up sexual frustration finally being released.

When she opened her eyes, Micah was staring at her with a look that she was sure mirrored hers. She noticed a look of wonderment and desire that she too was feeling for him.

"I know I keep saying this, but you are incredibly beautiful even after three rounds of tiring a brother out."

She laughed when he did.

"You shouldn't talk at all. I'm hoping once I do decide to move out of this bed, I'm still able to walk," she said.

"I hope I wasn't too rough on you. It's been quite some time for me."

"I should be asking you the same thing. I was pretty rough on you too."

Micah smiled.

"Yes you were and I loved it. I guess I shouldn't have let the bohemian, relaxed look fool me. In my private thoughts, I was wondering where you keep the whips and chains because sexually you are explosive!" he exclaimed.

Zora didn't know who she was either. He released a beast in her that she didn't know existed. Once they reached the bed, they started off in the middle with her legs spread open for him as he found his way to her center. Then they had somehow turned with her on top as he then turned to the opposite end of the bed. Before long, they were laying across it with her head hanging over the side as he plundered into her body over and over again with her legs high up on his shoulders, a position that brought her immeasurable joy and a level of pleasure she never knew existed.

"I never thought about whips and chains, but the visual you just gave me has me thinking all kinds of fun things I'd love to do to your incredible body. I should say I hope I wasn't too rough and wild on you. I found myself wanting to let go and holding nothing back. Is that crazy considering we really haven't known each other long?"

"It's not crazy at all. You were hot and I have no complaints. Being with you was fun, exciting and damn near intoxicating," Micah admitted.

"I don't know who that person was that was with you the past few hours. I could say it's unlike me, but since it was me I can't say that. I couldn't seem to get enough of you," Zora crooned.

"I want you to know that feeling is mutual," he added.

"I've wanted to strip you naked since the first time I saw you. I'm glad I didn't have to since you so willingly did so."

Laughter filled the room as the mood lightened. Zora moved forward as she felt the hand Micah had placed on her bare hip pull her closer to him.

"You're too far away," he whispered when she came close enough for him to capture her lips in a sensual kiss.

As he leaned into the kiss, he didn't know what was happening between them, especially since it was new and unexpected. He didn't know if this was just sex or if they were going to try for something more. For the moment, he enjoyed being with her and hoped she felt the same way. He also hoped she would be interested in finding out where this could lead. He wasn't the casual sex type of guy, though he wasn't sure he could convince her of that tonight.

Zora loved being with Micah like this. She had not shared her bed with a man since her husband. This was new territory for her and strangely, she felt comfortable.

She'd fought getting involved with anyone for a long time and now that she'd had sex with Micah, she felt free. She felt like she had been carrying a weight that had been lifted. She didn't know where this was leading, but she was more than willing to find out. She needed to be sure things wouldn't be awkward. His parents, after all, lived right next door. Speaking of that, she didn't know how he felt about being in her house in the light of day, with them noticing his car still outside.

"Micah, don't take this the wrong way, but I'm okay if you need to leave," she said snuggling closer to him, leaning into his embrace as he pulled her even closer him.

"Do you want me to leave Zora?" he asked, questionably.

"No Micah, I don't want you to leave. I just don't want things to be strange with your car being outside all night long and your parents living right next door. I wasn't sure what you wanted them to know or not to know and I don't want you feeling uncomfortable."

Micah kissed her softly on the lips before replying.

"I see what you mean. I'm supposed to pick Kaia up this morning early and I guess it would be strange being in the same clothes I dropped her off in, not to mention, leaving and possibly running into one of my parents. I guess I do need to leave because I also want to protect you. You are very close with my parents and until we know what's going on between us, I also don't want to be the cause of any awkwardness."

Zora appreciated his caring about how his

parents viewed her. She was hoping to get another round in before he left so she boldly rolled over until she was on top of him and slid her body over his until their most intimate parts were aligned.

"You don't have to leave just yet do you?" she asked sexily.

"I can't tell you how much I want to say no, but I need to say yes. I don't have any more condoms and I'm guessing you don't have any?" he asked hopeful.

Zora's thoughts of another round were deflated.

"No. I don't, but I can think of a few things we can do that doesn't involve them and if we find ourselves in this predicament again, I can assure you, there will be plenty in my nightstand."

Micah grinned. He knew that if it were up to him, they would be in this predicament again soon.

"I like how you think. I say we give those ideas a try before the sun comes up all the way up."

Micah grinded up into her and watched as Zora's eyes widened.

"I see the sun isn't the only thing coming up!"

Before Micah could respond, she slid down his body to show him what her other ideas were all about.

8

Zora didn't like that she had to keep the secret from Micah's parents that they were seeing each other. After the night they'd spent together following the party, they'd met several times for dinner and had indulged in several hot and sexy liaisons at his house. She never imagined that sex could be as wild and uninhibited as it was with him.

Tonight they were planning to spend an evening at her home without having to play cloak and dagger to avoid being seen by his parents. They were away on a trip for a few days and Kaia was spending a few days with her other grandparents.

She had spent the day getting ready for an evening of seduction that would test even her own limits. She loved that they enjoyed spending time together and that neither had any problems with the fact that dating and getting to know each other was fun, but the sex was taking a front seat to their time together. She knew that Micah wanted her to know that he wasn't only interested in her for the great sex they engaged in, but that he could never seem to get enough of her and she felt the same way.

She and Micah had talked the night before about letting his parents know that they've been seeing each other because they no longer wanted it to be a secret. He wanted Kaia to get to know her, a first for him and he knew his parents would be happy. She smiled when she remembered Micah telling her that though he had done some dating, he had never introduced any woman to his daughter before, making sure that no bonding would take place since he wasn't sure he had ever been ready for anything serious with any woman after Karen. Now they were talking of taking an evening to go out for some burgers and fries, something he had recently allowed Kaia to begin eating so that any reservations he'd previously had about Kaia seeing a woman around him could be put to rest.

Kaia had already gotten accustomed to seeing her at his parents' house since she was often there to visit with them and now Micah wanted her to see her with him. This was a big step after only a few weeks of dating, but she was more than ready for it. Micah was becoming more than just a casual fling to her and he had no problem letting her know that he was developing some pretty serious feelings for her. They would eventually get around to talking more about where the relationship was going, but tonight, she wanted to focus on their pleasure and the fun they would have after a long week of work.

She smiled thinking of the special plans she had for them tonight. She discovered that though they both had not been intimate with anyone since the passing of their spouses, they loved being adventurous when it came to sex. Tonight, she was looking forward to a new experience.

While shopping online for paint supplies a week ago, she discovered a link to paints that had nothing to do with the kind of art she taught. When she saw a website that boasted about their edible paint, she had no idea the site was related to intimacy and what she discovered had images of Micah covered in body paint right before she began licking it slowly off. Before she second guess her decision, she'd ordered a few tubes and impatiently waited for them to be delivered.

The night was going to be a special one after she stopped at Victoria's Secret on her way home and purchased the cutest pink and black two piece set with a barely there thong that was held together by two thin pieces of string. The set also included a bra with tiny cups that barely covered her large breasts, but that's the way she wanted it. She loved the tease the tiny cups provided and knew Micah would love it. If she knew nothing else, she knew that Micah was a breast man from the many times he'd told her about his dreams about them when she wasn't around and the way he fondled them every time he got the opportunity.

Now she was checking on the set-up for her evening of love. She had set up a mattress in her art studio and placed battery operated candles all around the room. There was too much real paint on this level for real candles and she didn't want to start a fire that was the kind that radiated from their bodies. There were enough flames when the two of them got together.

Zora looked around the room at her handy work, including the silver tray filled with chocolate covered strawberries, an aphrodisiac that was sure to keep the sexy night going all night long and some cheeses for when they actually did get hungry.

She walked passed a mirror and checked her attire, already donning the sexy lingerie under the silk robe she was now wearing. She was making one last glance around the room at her handy work when the doorbell chime.

Zora pulled the black satin robe tighter around her body and headed to let Micah in. As she opened the door, her body tingled at the sight of him standing in her doorway looking like a sexy male model. She slowly licked her lips and with her index finger, signaled for him to enter, knowing she was looking forward to him entering more than just her door.

Micah felt like his tongue had gone numb when

Zora opened the door and stood before him in a short black robe with only a sash holding it together. He tried with his mind to will the sash to fall open, but he had no such luck. He looked from her feet which were encased in sexy strappy heels and moved his eyes painstakingly slow up her body until he reached her cleavage which peeped out from beneath her robe getting his fill, wondering how long he would have to wait until he could see what was underneath.

Zora looked like a seductress and he felt like he had just entered her lair. His body hardened and he had to adjust his stance in order to accommodate the rising hard-on that pressed against the inside of his zipper. He loved how she never ceased to amaze him with her loveliness and her ability to literally get a rise out of him every time he laid eyes on her.

"Should I be scared to come in tonight?" he asked with a voice laden with raw passion.

Zora stepped back to let him in.

"Never be scared to enter my domain. There is always pleasure on this side of the door for you."

"In that case, I'm here," he said excitedly.

Zora noticed he had two bags. One she knew was an overnight bag since they had decided he should stay the night. The other she wasn't too sure of.

"What's in the other bag?"

Micah looked down at the bag he was carrying, almost forgetting he had it.

"Oh, right, I stopped on my way here and picked

up a few movies, but I'm beginning to think I won't need them."

"No, you won't need them unless they're x-rated. Otherwise, they are definitely a waste of time, at least tonight," she said saucily.

Micah caught on quick. He was nothing if he was not perceptive.

"Well I'll just leave these movies here at the door and will gladly take them back tomorrow," he said slyly to happily go along with the plans Zora had for the evening.

"Tonight, Mr. Prentiss, is all about pleasure, yours and mine. We are venturing up to the top level to my studio tonight. Why don't you go ahead and get comfortable and meet me there when you're ready. Just in case you're wondering what the attire is for the night, may I suggest you come naked?"

Zora didn't bat an eye making sure Micah knew that they were going to have a good time and she was more than serious about him getting out of every stitch of clothing that he'd shown up in.

"Baby, if you stand here long enough, you'll get naked Micah in about one minute," he admitted.

"Mmmm, I really like how you think. I know you didn't have long after you got off work to do much other than pick up and drop Kaia off, so I left fresh linens in the bathroom if you'd like to shower. I'm going to go up and make sure things are ready for our night of pure, unadulterated pleasure."

Micah grabbed one last kiss and a handful of her behind before slowing things down and going to undress and shower. He was looking forward to unwinding.

Zora had just finished filling the last bowl with the tasty edible paint. Her excitement was building up by the second with what she had planned for Micah. Getting the paint was a great idea. She had selected four flavors from the many options the website had available. Yellow was banana flavored and she couldn't wait to try it out on Micah's banana, she thought to herself, smiling and licking her lips imagining she already had him under her touch. Next there was the red edible paint that was a strawberry flavor and the exciting factor was strawberry was her favorite flavor. The last two were green and purple, with the green being apple flavored, while the purple was a grape flavor which according to the description would remind her of grape candy she'd loved as a child. She couldn't wait to taste them all as she poured herself a glass of wine and waited.

9

Micah had finished his shower and was walking into Zora's studio just as she was bending over to place the last bowl on the floor by a mattress he noticed she had placed in the center of the room. His eyes widened as he got a glimpse of what he knew was waiting for him and just as his body did when he first arrived, he hardened and reached down to first stroke himself lightly before readjusting his member to a more comfortable position under the towel he'd wrapped around his hips.

He looked around the studio and noticed that Zora had moved all of her easels so that they were against the wall and she had centered the mattress and placed electric candles all around the room. He knew this was definitely a setting for seduction and he was more than ready. The bowls on the floor seemed odd and out of place since they weren't filled with food, but with some type of colored liquid. As he got closer, he tried to catch a whiff thinking it may be paint, but the smell was fruity.

"Zora, baby, what's up with the bowls on the floor?" he asked.

Zora looked back at him as she continued setting up the scene.

"It's paint I picked up just for you."

"Paint? I'm going to be painting?" he asked.

"No, you're going to be painted. This is edible body paint."

"Are you serious? Edible paint?"

"Yes? Are you concerned?" she said laughing.

"No concern on my part."

"Don't worry. I promise you will enjoy what I have planned."

Micah trusted her completely.

"I'm not concerned. See, this is me not being concerned," he said making sure he showed a relaxed look on his face.

"Come here," she said.

Micah went closer and noticed that she also had various fruits and some wine chilling on ice with two glasses already poured and ready. When he came close enough to reach for her, he pulled her close, flush with his already hardening body.

"I've missed you today," he said, in a deep and sultry voiced laced with more than a subtle hit of desire for her. Where he would normally go straight for her lips, he instead leaned into her neck, placing a soft kiss there.

When Zora leaned further into his embrace, he added more kisses, some open mouthed and others where he added a nibble at the end. When he felt her body tremble, he knew he was hitting all of the perfect spots.

"I've missed you too," she whispered breathlessly.

"Baby, thank you for planning this night together for us. I've had a crazy week at the station and all day long, I looked forward to getting over here to you to have you in my arms just like this," he crooned while stroking her back lightly through her robe.

"As you can see I was just as excited about the night we would get to spend together. I know I've been a little busy finishing up my pieces for the showcase and I wanted you to know just how much I had missed you."

"We both have work that takes up a lot of our time and right now, this time is all about you and me and that's it. How does that sound?"

Zora nodded, not being able to find the words once Micah leaned back and looked down into her eyes. In what seemed like slow motion, he leaned down and captured her lips and didn't wait before seeking entry into her mouth where his tongue went in search of hers for the tango she had grown accustomed to. The experience was electrifying and she held on tight to his shoulders as he went deeper as if he were unable to get enough of her. The sound of their mutual moans was a turn-on and she was glad she hadn't added music to the ambiance because all she wanted to hear and feel was Micah.

Micah couldn't wait any longer to see what was under Zora's short robe. He broke off the kiss as he untied the sash that held the sides together. As the robe fell away, he got his first look and was speechless. He had never seen such a beautiful sight and he marveled at her flawless beauty.

"You look hot baby," he said. "This is all for me?" he asked.

Zora smiled at his jubilance, appreciative that he never misses an opportunity to let her know how beholden he is with her.

"Yes, sweetheart, everything you see in front of you is all for you."

Micah reached to bring her back close to him again when she halted him.

Zora knew what was next, but she wanted to slow things down a bit because they had all night and she had plans.

"Come lie down on the mattress and let me explain what's on the menu tonight besides me, of course."

He followed along ready to do anything she asked at this point. She wanted to lead tonight and he had no problem following.

"I have some wine and fruit because it's something we both love along with a variety of cheeses, but new for tonight is what's in the bowls. I told you they were edible paints and tonight I want you to lay down, relax and let me turn this seduction up a few notches."

As he made himself comfortable on the mattress, or as comfortable as he could be with a raging hard-on, Micah tried to pay attention to what she was saying, but all he could focus on was the outfit she was wearing. It was pink and black and unless he was imagining things, it was also see through in the right places that allowed him to see the dark circles of her nipples and when he looked down further, he saw a thing dark line of hair on her mound that looked like a path showing him where he knew he wanted to be. His tongue felt heavy in his mouth and his body felt an undying urge to merge with hers, but he didn't act on it, allowing her to take control of their lovemaking and whatever she had planned that would leave up to it.

Zora noticed he wasn't listening to her explain about her plan. She knew the lingerie would be a hit and if the look on his face was any sign, she had hit jackpot with this one.

"Micah, did you hear me?" she nudged, causing him to again focus on her words and not her body.

"What?"

He hadn't heard anything because the visual had his attention.

"I was explaining the bowls to you."

"Oh, I'm sorry sweetheart, but this lingerie you

have on stole my attention and your words suddenly faded away, but I'm back now so go ahead and continue. I know you said the paints were edible so I do remember that, but can you talk a little faster so that I can have a chance to enjoy all of this before a brother has a heart attack. Your teasing game is on point and I feel like a moth drawn to a flame and in any second, I'm going to combust right here and what I want is to be inside of you."

Micah reached for her and Zora moved out of the way knowing that if he touched her, she would give in and she'd be naked, writhing around under him and she wanted to reserve that for a little later.

She waved her finger back and forth at him letting him know it wasn't time for that yet, as much as she really wanted it.

"Not yet, lover boy. We have the entire night and I intend for us to be exhausted come daylight."

Micah smiled ready for just about anything she was dishing up for him.

"Okay, I'm sorry, baby. I'm listening so continue on," he said leaning over, bracing himself on an elbow to be sure he was giving her his full attention.

"The paints, Micah, are edible and quite flavorful according to the thousands of online reviews I read about them."

"Now that sounds tasty. I hope you're not the only one who will get a taste tonight."

Micah's eyes followed her every move as he

watched her reach a finger into the bowl with the red paint in it, drew up a little paint on her finger and swiped it across his lips. Before her finger had barely left his lips, he stuck his tongue out to get a taste and his penis stiffened even harder as a sudden rush of flavor seeped through his body. The paint didn't just taste sweet, but if erotic had a flavor, this would be it.

"That's delicious," he said on a groan as he made sure he licked up every drop.

"I thought you'd like that and the hungry look in your eyes says it all. I'm figuring we can spend the evening testing and tasting what's in the bowls by painting each other and licking it off."

"I like how you think baby."

"I'm thinking that by the end of the night, you'll also like how I taste," she added.

"Considering I already love how you taste, I can see I'll be close to that heart attack I mentioned if I get to spread this all over you and then like a hungry man at a buffet, I get to lick it from every part of your luscious body. I'm all for that, so let's start with you first," he said reaching for her.

This time Zora went into his arms, unable to resist the heated, hooded, sexual gaze from his eyes. Micah, not being able to wait any longer, reached for Zora and tumbled her on the mattress until she was under him.

Before he leaned down to cover her body with his, she held her arms stiff, holding him off.

"I wanted to start with you to show you a night of seduction. You always take care of me when we're intimate, making sure that my needs are met way before yours and several times over I might add. I wanted this night to be about you."

"You're right baby and I'm sorry. I'm so hot and excited when I'm around you that patience takes a back seat. I am always accommodating when it comes to you and you had this night planned. I'm going to do as you ask and let you have your way with me, but just to be on the safe side, do you have a defibrillator around here someplace because you may need it to revive me several times," he quipped, causing Zora to laugh out loud.

Micah rolled so that Zora was now on top as he placed his hands behind his head to show her that she was in control. The towel that he'd wrapped around his hips had now come off and he knew she could see how hard it was for him to keep from getting inside of her immediately.

Zora saw how ready Micah was for her and she had to slow her heart rate, tamper down her breathing and get back to the night she had planned and soon enough, she'd give them both what they wanted and needed.

Zora got her fill of the fine specimen in front of her and no longer able to resist, she reached out and slid her hands across his taut, muscular chest, going up and around his shoulders and then down his bulging arms.

"Close our eyes and enjoy," she uttered as she leaned over and placed a soft kiss on his chest.

Zora smiled when he followed her instruction, relaxed and allowed her to have her way with him. She removed the towel from under his hips and placed a soft, sweet kiss on his left hip. Micah hadn't expected that, causing him to groan at the contact and she smiled at his reaction to her.

"You're killing me slowly, baby," he expressed, barely able to get the words out and trying hard to maintain control.

Zora chuckled again enjoying the hold she now has over him. She felt invigorated and powerful and all she wanted to do was please him as he always does with her. Not waiting any longer, she reached into the strawberry flavored paint and painted a path from his chin all the way to the patch of hair right above his extremely hard, long and thick penis. He had the body of a god and she could look at him naked like this all day and never tire. She dipped her hand into the bowl of yellow paint, which was the banana flavored and smeared it all over Micah's banana from root to the large mushroom head, that night after night, brought her so much pleasure. She was already satisfied with her work and began her descent down his body. She first started at his chin and kissed all around his neck, getting groans and moans from him, letting her know that he loved what she was doing to him. He was about to move his hands from behind his head and probably grab for her and Zora stopped him.

"Just relax and enjoy baby. Now you see how it feels when you slowly tease me to a point that I can hardly breathe. You look delicious all painted up in front of me. You know how much I love my art and adding you to it has not allowed me to derive a whole new level of respect for my craft and for your delicious body."

Without any further words, she licked her way down the path of the strawberry flavored paint adding kisses in with her licks down his body.

Micah moved around on the mattress under Zora ministrations and delighted in the pleasure of her kisses and licks. His body was on fire and he knew that any minute, he would implode on the spot, giving in to his body's desire for release

"So far, very good baby. Your body mixed with strawberries is better than any dessert I could ever ask for."

He opened his eyes and looked at Zora as she used her finger to capture residue of paint from her lips and placed it in her mouth. That was the most erotic thing he'd ever seen. He was about to tell her so when all breath left his body. Before he could get a word out of his mouth, Zora, keeping her eyes on his, leaned down and took his paint covered member into her mouth without any warning to him at all that her intent was to do that. He was so caught up in hearing her talk and knowing she was making her way towards his erection, he thought she would take her time, but she didn't.

Zora watched as Micah's mouth formed and "o" and he once again closed his eyes. She didn't give him time to catch his breath. She took as much of him as she could into her mouth only going about half way before pulling him out to the tip and then going back down on him again. Loving her man like this, with him allowing her to pleasure him while he laid back and just enjoyed her caresses was all she needed and wanted. She closed her eyes and gave her all to satisfying him.

Micah felt like he was floating as Zora took him in with deep plunges, causing his hips to uncontrollably jerk up to meet her downward lunges. She didn't take him slowly or gently, but instead, she went at him like a starving woman. She sucked him in, then licked more of the banana flavored paint off of him, and then sucked him in again.

Zora was not herself. She was a sex goddess who was setting out to bring her man the ultimate in pleasure and by his reaction, she was doing just that.

Micah could feel it happening and before he could gather his thoughts and prepare for the imminent explosion, his body shot off like a rocket as an orgasm slammed into him like none he'd ever experienced before. He saw stars and heard rockets and screamed though he tried to suppress the sound. Zora continued to stroke and lick him until his body calmed down from the raging waves that had rocked his body. When he could breathe and see again, he opened his eyes and brought Zora up so that she was face to face with him and he kissed her deeply, showing his appreciation for the pleasure.

"No words can describe how you make me feel and since I'm talking, I'll assume I didn't suffer a heart attack, but I felt like I was on the brink of one."

He kissed her again and this time he removed the robe from her shoulders.

"It's your turn, baby," he whispered as he moved so that she was now laying on the mattress and he covered her body with his, kissing her lips, her face and around her neck as he reached for the paint bowls.

Micah wanted to remove the lingerie, but for the moment, he wanted to leave it on her. Without giving her a chance to speak, he reached into bowl of purple paint and covered all five of his fingers with it. He smeared one finger across her lips, coating them and used another to place some paint on each nipple through the sheer cups of her bra. He smeared the remaining paint on her exposed abdomen and stomach. He then reached into the bowl with the green paint, coating his fingers once again and reached to coat the area between her legs with the apple scented paint, again right through the sheer lace of her panties. He would remove both soon, but for now, he wanted to feel and taste her through the fabric.

"Enjoy baby," he stated right before he took her mouth and plunged relentlessly into it, getting and giving everything, letting her feel his need for her in his kiss.

Micah slid further down her body until he was eye level with her breasts. He first licked the nipples through the lace until they were hard, marbled peaks and then he sucked as much of one breast into his mouth as he could get while he caressed the other with his hand. Her globes felt large and heavy and the weight of them excited him even more.

He then slid his hand from her breast to the area between her legs where he spread the paint all around the lace and without warning, he slipped a finger beyond the lace and into her slippery tunnel. He knew Zora hadn't been expecting that and when her body leaped up off of the mattress, he knew it was the right move. As she squirmed around under him, he moved even further down her body and allowed his tongue to join his finger. He licked some of the paint from her panties, stroking her and enjoying the smell of her essence mixed in with the fruity smell of the paint. Not being able to resist anymore, he slid the now soaked panties from her body, tossing them aside and laid flat on his stomach while spreading her legs wide at the same time. He reached for any bowl of paint, not caring the flavor and rubbed some all around the apex of her thighs and before Zora could get her next breath out, he slipped his tongue inside of her, using his finger to tease the hard nub and before long, he felt Zora fly off the edge into an orgasmic bliss and he continue to feast until her hips stopped gyrating and she collapsed hard down on the mattress.

"That's it baby, give me all of it," he said in between licks and sucks.

Zora was trying to survive the feeling, but the talking was her undoing as a second orgasm slammed into her so quickly she didn't have a chance to catch her breath from the first one. When Micah reached up and caressed her breasts just the way she like, pinching her nipples while rubbing the grape scented edible paint all over them, she lost all ability to think as she reached down and grabbed a hold of his head to keep him from going anywhere as she rode out her second climax on his tongue.

Micah's excitement went to a whole other level when Zora reached down to hold his head in place, as if he was thinking of going anyplace. Her shout of pleasure rocked his world and seeing her in the midst of her orgasm was the best sight from his viewpoint. He kept his eyes on her until her body finally did simmer down.

Micah slid slowly up so that his body covered her and whispered in her ear.

"I need more baby. Are you ready for more?" he asked. Zora couldn't speak, but she nodded her head in agreement. She could never have too much of him.

Micah reached over and opened up one of the condoms Zora had laid out and after covering his pulsating flesh, which was more than ready for the next round, he reached down, drew her legs up and around his hips and he entered her as they cried out from the pure pleasure of the intimate connection. As Zora wrapped her legs around his back, he reached down to grip her behind in his hands so that he could go as deep as possible.

He set first a slow, deep penetrating pace and as Zora pushed up to meet his downward strokes, he increased the pace as they raced together for the ledge and before long, they tumbled over it into a sexual bliss.

Zora had never felt so alive in her life and never before had she had three orgasm, one right after the other. She realized it wasn't just the intimacy that did this for her, but it was Micah himself. He brought something new and fresh into her life and she welcomed it. She never thought she'd feel this way about another man again and was happy that she took a leap and decided to go with her feelings and not live in the past anymore. Tonight she put her all into being with him. She wanted to show him that he meant everything to her and she would do anything for him. Tonight they had come together as one and not just in a sexual way because it was far beyond that. Sex was only one aspect of what they had together. Putting anything sexual on the side, she already knew she was in love again.

Micah had one thought in mind as he withdrew from her body, pulled her closely into him and slipped into an exhaustive sleep. This wasn't just lust, it was love.

10

The morning came quicker than Micah and Zora thought. They had spent the entire night making love and after moving from her studio to her bedroom sometime in the middle of the night, they continued until neither of move a muscle. They had taken a quick nap earlier and when Zora woke to the most amazing feeling of kisses being placed across her back, she leaned back into Micah and enjoyed the close connection. They had both awakened to a hunger that with all of the lovemaking, they hadn't remembered to feed and that was one that actually involved food.

They had agreed it was time to move the fun to the bedroom and while she cleaned up, Micah moved the fruit and cheeses that she had laid out to the bedroom and went to the kitchen in search of food that would build their energy back up. He found the makings for some sandwiches and by the time he had made them, Zora was already running a shower for them to wash off the paint.

After making love in the shower, they finally got around to eating the food and after one last exhaustive round of sex, they had finally fallen asleep in each other's arms.

Now it was morning and as much as they would like to, they needed to get up because Zora had a lot of work to do in order to continue preparing for her upcoming art exhibit.

She went to move from within Micah's embrace when she felt herself being pulled back in.

"Good morning to you too," she said, turning so that they were facing each other.

Micah leaned over and placed a soft kiss on her lips.

"Thank you for an incredible evening and yes, good morning. Are you as exhausted as I am because you made a brother work overtime all night long," he chuckled before kissing her again.

"Oh, there is enough exhaustion to go around this morning. You were insatiable last night so you should be tired. I'm surprised I'm able to move this morning."

"I can recall you not letting up on me all night long and just in case there was any doubt, I loved all of it."

Zora put a sad look on her face.

"Now it's over because I have to get up and finish

working on the pieces for my gallery showing."

"Am I invited to this showing I keep hearing so much about? My mother mentioned it last week and I think she was fishing to see if perhaps you had mentioned it to me."

"Of course you're invited and I suspect your mother is not as clueless as we think. Do you think it's time to tell them about us?"

Micah reached for Zora and put on his serious face.

"I now realize we should have told them weeks ago when we first started seeing each other. I knew then that I was drawn to you and that if we started something, there was no way I was going to let you go, so there was no need to keep anything from my parents. I don't even remember why we decided to do that, but now, I think it's time we let them know. I have no doubt they'll be happy and like you, I believe my mother already knows something and just hasn't said anything."

"It's been hard keeping this from your mother because I respect her and we're very close, but I know we agreed to keep it between us in case things didn't work out and there would be less people involved, but I knew from the moment I met you that you would be someone special to me and I can't begin to tell you how happy I am that we are together."

Micah didn't want to hold back what was in his heart and also on the tip of his tongue.

"Zora, baby, I love you and if you think it's too soon to say that because it's only been about six weeks that we've been seeing each other, I want you to know that I don't take love lightly and I don't toss it out because of great sex. You are an incredible woman and I'm happy every time we're together and when we're not, I'm thinking about you all the time."

"I love you too," Zora said with unshed tears in her eyes.

"Don't cry baby," Micah said as one tear fell from her eye and rested on her cheek.

"I haven't been this happy in a very long time and it's because you brought love back in my life and any woman would be lucky to have a great man like you. There is never a point where falling in love is done too fast as long as it's right and the love that's received is also given and I do very much love you too."

They kissed and after expressing their love for each other, the kiss felt like it was brand new. Now that they were in love, it was brand new. The kiss was an exchange of the beginning of what they each hoped would be forever. Micah had an idea.

"Just how busy is your day today?" he asked.

"My morning is pretty busy putting final touches on a few pieces for the showing, but my late afternoon and evening are pretty open. What did you have in mind?"

"I'm meeting some friends later on for drinks

and dinner and I want you to join me. My parents won't be back until tomorrow so we can tell them about us then but tonight, I want my friends to meet the woman I love. Are you up for it?" he asked.

"Yes I am. I look forward to meeting these friends you talk about all the time. I especially can't wait to meet your best friend who lives in Baltimore one day."

Zora moved so that she was sitting up in bed and facing Micah who had now done the same thing.

"We're doing this aren't we? We're in love."

Micah leaned over and placed a soft kiss on her lips.

"Yes, baby, we are and I couldn't be more happy. You go ahead and get a shower while I straighten up a bit. I would join you, but if I did, you would never get anything done today."

Zora smiled and after checking the time, knew he was right. She needed to shower and do it alone and then get to work. They had a full day ahead of them. She unashamedly left the bed in all of her nakedness and walked to the adjoining bathroom to shower.

"You're trying to tempt a brother aren't you? If I didn't know that you had a deadline, that little walk of yours all naked and sexy would already have me following you, but I'm going to think about the weather or sports or something to keep my mind off of you being in that shower all lathered up and slippery."

Zora smiled, blew a kiss at him and closed the bathroom door behind her.

**

Zora can't remember a time when she'd been this nervous before. She wasn't this nervous meeting Micah's friends the night before, but today, knowing that any minute, she and Micah would be telling his parents that they were in love. She wasn't nervous thinking that they wouldn't be receptive to it, but her nervousness derived from the fact that they had kept the fact that they were seeing each other from his parents for so long.

Micah was first stopping at his in-laws' house to pick up Kaia and then he was going to call her when he pulled up in front of the brownstone. They were planning to show up at his parents' house together to share the good news.

She put aside being nervous to smile at how wonderful the night before had been. Micah's friends were nice and fun to be around and they received her as if she had always been a part of their circle. These were friends Micah had before he and his wife had moved from Boston and began their life in Baltimore. All of them had known and loved Karen and not one had tried to compare them, but they each told her how happy they could see that Micah has been since they had begun seeing each other. That comment made her glow all evening and she was able to relax and join in on the dinner conversation. They had enjoyed an early dinner and since the night was still young, they decided to go back to Micah's house for an evening of game board and card playing. Micah had put out finger food while she put everything out for drinks, including coffee. At one point, she looked around the kitchen and realized they looked like an old married couple prepping for an evening of guests. Micah must have noticed the same thing because he turned to her and said exactly what she had been thinking.

At the end of the night, she was victorious at playing spades having played it many times in the past. Charades was not her game to play and she and Micah laughed at the fact that though she sucked at the game, he was able to guess a lot of what she was trying to mimic and according to his friends, that was the makings of a great relationship and she couldn't agree more.

Now she paced around her living room with sweaty palms and shaky legs hoping that Micah's mother isn't too upset with her keeping the secret. Her phone rang, shaking her out of her nervousness.

"I'm pulling up into a parking space in front of the house," Micah said when she answered.

"Okay, I'm coming out," she declared, knowing her time of waiting was over.

Zora grabbed her things and went out the door where she saw a waiting Micah and Kaia at the foot of her steps. After locking the door she spoke first to Kaia who grinned at her before shyly tucking her head into her father's shoulder.

"Are you ready?" Micah asked noticing her nervousness.

"I would say no, but it's too late to be nervous now."

"I love you Zora and my parents love you like a daughter and I know everything is going to be fine. Don't be nervous."

Zora smiled finding peace in Micah's face and in his words meant to comfort her.

"I love you too. Let's go," she said leading the way to his parents steps.

Micah used his key to open the door and called out to his parents once they were all in.

"Mom, Dad are you here?" he asked, looking around, finding them in the kitchen.

When they entered his mother immediately reached for Kaia who instantly held her arms out to be picked from Micah's arms. She then smiled with delight when she saw Zora step into the room behind Micah.

"Zora, so nice to see you. I haven't seen you in almost a week. I assume you've been preparing for the art show which I'm extremely excited about."

Zora gave her a hug and a quick kiss on the cheek and stepped around her to give Micah's dad a quick hug as well.

"Yes, the showing has me on pins and needles these days and I'm just about ready. I have a courier coming tomorrow to begin transporting my pieces to the museum and next week, I'll spend a lot of time there setting each piece in exactly the right place. I've been working on the layout and I believe I'm just about done. How was your trip away?" she asked, trying to find a comfortable conversation to ease her apprehension.

"Before I get into that, would you like anything to drink or perhaps a muffin? I just took some blueberry one's out of the oven and one apple muffin for Kaia to nibble on."

Zora looked to Micah and then back to his mother.

"A muffin would be nice. Why don't I get them since you have Kaia in your arms and I'm sure she's not going to let you put her down since she's probably missed seeing you the past few days."

Micah knew it was time to clear the air so that Zora could breathe freely.

"Mom, Dad I'm glad you both had a great time on your trip and before we get into the two of you telling us all about it, I have something I'd like to talk to you about."

His father turned toward him first and after placing Kaia in her high-chair at the table, his mother turned to him as well. He noticed a look of concern on her face and assumed he was about to bring them some bad news.

"What's wrong son?"

"Mom, nothing is wrong and in fact, everything

is right. Let me dive right in without dragging this out too long. Zora and I have been seeing each other since the night of the welcome to Boston party you gave and I wanted you and Pop to know that I'm in love with her."

He watched as his mother turned to Zora before turning back to him.

"Whew, Micah, you are certainly one for the dramatics. The look you had on your face made me think something was wrong you looked so serious. Just so that both of you know, I already knew and I told your father that I thought something was going on."

"I told you she probably knew, Micah," Zora said after placing the muffins on the table.

"Of course I knew. Anyone in attendance at the party that night would have to be blind to not see the connection the two of you had and I knew that nothing was going to keep the two of you apart."

"We thought you'd be upset that we haven't told you earlier than now," Micah added.

"I'm far from upset and your personal life is yours. I'm just glad you finally did let us in on it so that I could openly tell Zora that I'm happy for you both and that she's always felt like a daughter to us and now that the two of you are together, I don't have to keep wondering if my prediction was true or not."

Zora, overwhelmed with glee gave her a hug and went around to hug Micah's father as well.

"Thanks Mom for understanding. Zora and I weren't sure of where we were headed, but now that we're in love, we want everyone to know and share in our love."

"Son, love is meant to be shared with those around you and for the first time in a long time, I have seen how happy you have been lately and that alone makes me happy. Now, let's sit down and enjoy a few muffins and some coffee and let me tell you and Zora all about our trip while your father gets the gifts we brought back, especially for my baby here."

Micah walked over and kissed Zora softly on the cheek happy that he could openly show his love and affection for her and out of the corner of his eye, he saw his mother smile.

11

Finally the night of her art showcase had arrived and it was a night of who is who in the art world around the Boston area. According to the museum director, there were also guests from around the country and some from as far away as Paris, to her surprise. Zora recognized a few of her guests from out of the country, especially those who had contracted her in the past to paint for them.

"I take it that's Micah?" Zora's friend Sheila asked as she sidled up next to her.

Zora looked in the direction that Sheila was looking and saw the love of her life lighting up the room with his sexiness in a black tuxedo looking as if it had been crafted and put together just for him.

"Yes it is. That's him and isn't he gorgeous?"

"I see he has you smiling like a Cheshire cat and yes he is. I'm extremely happy for you."

"I can't help, but smile whenever I think about

him and especially every time I see him."

"I couldn't miss the way he was devouring you with his eyes. All this hotness up in here tonight between the two of you. Go get a room already!" Sheila exclaimed.

"Oh, that's definitely in my plans for later on."

They laughed and Sheila hugged her around the shoulders.

"I guess I don't have to worry about hooking you up with anyone anymore, huh?"

"No She, you don't. I have all the man I need right there in that fine specimen you see across the room."

Zora continued watching as Micah escorted his mom on his arm making their way from one art piece to the next and in between, greeting and welcoming guests. She was sad that his father was unable to make it, but Kaia had come down with a little fever and he opted to stay home and look after her so that Micah and his mom could come to the showing and she was glad when she looked up and saw him coming through the door earlier. She had been at the gallery all day and when he called to tell her Kaia was sick, she told him it would be okay if he missed her showing. He dismissed her offer and told her he would not miss her opening and that, yes, Kaia meant everything to him, but now so did she and that his father had already volunteered to look after her and even Karen's parents had offered to watch her so that Micah could enjoy an evening celebrating her. He told her that they were just as happy to hear that he was in love again as his parents were and now they all felt like one big happy family which now included her.

Zora was pleased with how the night had turned out. Throughout the night, Micah had come by to check on her and when they could, they greeted her guests together as a couple. Just about every piece of art she showcased had been purchased and she knew she would soon be busy again painting new pieces. She had spent months planning for this showcase and she was happy with the pieces she'd decided to display.

She was proud of the successful showing and was overwhelmed with joy that her most personal and private piece of art, which was her portrait of Isaac in his military uniform, was finally unveiled. She had been working on it for years and remembered how hard it was to get it finished without breaking out into uncontrollable tears to the point that she would have to cover it up and take weeks and sometimes months to go back to it.

Her love for him and the love that she now felt for Micah was her greatest inspiration to put all the pain in the past, embrace the now and look forward to the future. She still loved Isaac very much, but the pain of losing him lessened more and more everyday now that her life was being filled once again with love and happiness. She had not been planning to sell that piece because it was her prized possession, but she decided if someone wanted it, she would part with it. When she first saw the "sold" sign on it, she was nervous about someone else having that piece. She knew that if it sold, it was meant to be sold, so she decided to let it go. She had also painted a smaller version similar to the larger one of him and she would one day soon package it up and mail it to his family. She knew they would love to have it.

They were coming to the part of the evening when she would get to say thank you to all of those who had been supportive of the showcase. She excused herself from Sheila who had come to check on her after seeing the painting of Isaac unveiled knowing it had to have been hard on her and made her way to the podium in the main room of the gallery where everyone was gathering. She looked out and saw some of her closest friends including Sheila and her husband Barry and some of the teachers from the school where she taught art. She looked out just as Micah's mother blew her a kiss, showing her support as well. She was especially excited that she was able to fly her grandmother out for the showcase and she smiled when her grandmother waved letting her know how proud she was. The night was made perfect by her presence. Of course, her eyes landed upon Micah, the man of her dreams, the man who had captured her heart and the man whom she loved very much.

"Good evening everyone," she began. "I want to

thank each of you for coming out tonight to support this showcase. This was an especially difficult showcase because each of the pieces was born from a place in my life where there was much hurt. Most of these were painted with tears running down my face and not just tears of sadness, but tears of joy as well. Painting them helped me release a lot of pain and anguish over what I thought was me being dealt a bad hand in life. I now realize it was part of my awakening and I needed to do these paintings of my parents and my husband who passed away several years ago."

Zora paused as she prepared to give special thanks and hoped she could make it through without crying.

"I want to thank those closest to me for being here tonight and for doing any and everything to support me. My best friends, Sheila and her husband Barry are here. I met them when I first moved to Boston after I became the teacher to their oldest child and Sheila and I became friends instantly. I love you both and I thank you for being my rock. I see so many of the teachers from the school where I teach and I appreciate them coming out to show support as well. You can't help but develop a friendship with those who value the importance of educating the children, showing them how to appreciate all that they learn, showing them that we do what we do to prepare them for a life with a future and that life should be filled with art. My neighbor Ms. Sandra Prentiss is also here. She has been a mother figure since I arrived in Boston. I met her and her husband my first day here and not long after the movers had moved in the last piece of furniture, she knocked on my door with a plate of brownies, welcoming me to the neighborhood. I'm thankful for her today. I also want to thank the gallery owners for allowing my showcase today. They did an incredible job setting everything up including the food and the incredible decorations."

Everyone applauded at this point.

"To my grandmother who is also here tonight, I wouldn't be who I am if it were not for you. You didn't hesitate to take care of me when mom and dad died. I'm hoping that I have always made you proud."

Zora felt the tears about to flow when she saw her grandmother cry as well.

There was more applause while she tried to gather herself to continue.

Zora waited until the applause died down before finding the eyes of the man who meant the world to her.

"I want to give one very special thank you and it's my last, but certainly not my least. I want to thank my boyfriend, Micah."

Everyone looked at him while she struggled through her thank you to him. More tears began running down as she tried to get through it. She noticed him making his way closer to her, probably trying to get to her to console her. He didn't come up on the stage with her, but he remained close by in case she needed his closeness.

"I had been in such a bad space for a long time after the death of my husband. I put my focus on work and art and I stayed away from dating and friends trying to set me up on dates because I didn't think I was ready to open my heart up again. Then came Micah and he came into my life like a force. From the first day we met, I think I knew we were meant to be together and he along with his beautiful daughter, has helped bring the sunshine back into my life. Micah, baby, I love you and thank you for showing me that I can love unconditionally again without fear."

Micah knew the words she was saying were true because he felt the same way. He didn't want to see her cry and he really didn't want to make her cry so he just mouthed back to her that he loved her too, blew her a kiss and winked. When she smiled back, he knew she was going to be okay.

"Now everyone, continue to mingle and again, thank you for coming out tonight. I am blessed by your purchases and I look forward to seeing you all at another of my showcases."

Everyone applauded as she descended from the stage and into the arms of the man she loved. It was a perfect night.

12

Zora was happy to be home, working her way out of her evening gown. She didn't really like the glitzy, glamour life or clothing, but she had to admit that she loved the very formal off white gown she had on.

She and Sheila had gone shopping and had found the perfect gown just for her and the moment she saw it, she knew it was the one for her. She didn't always feel comfortable in black tie attire, but tonight warranted it. She felt lovely and from the looks Micah gave her all night, she was.

Micah had just come into her house after making sure his mother had gotten in okay and to check on his daughter. His dad had called to say her fever had broken earlier and she was asking for apples. Her grandmother was fast asleep in the guest room on the lower level, worn out from really enjoying herself. Micah told her he wanted to talk to her so he would stop over once he saw his mom home. She was exhausted, but never too tired when it came to him. Even now her thoughts turned to the other night where they had licked, eaten and sucked edible paint from each other's bodies. She had just finished putting on comfortable silk pajamas when she heard him enter the door she'd left unlocked for him. He was still in his tux with the tie missing. He looked tired and she could tell that he was worn out from the exciting evening. He wasn't planning to stay over since her grandmother was in the house, but she needed to see him before he went home as much as he needed to see her. She looked and noticed that he was carrying a covered canvas in his hands. He must have purchased a painting for his home tonight and he'd wanted to show it to her.

"Baby I'm not going to stay long. I just wanted to see you before I went home. I'm looking at you right now and all I can think about is crawling in bed with you, but I know neither one of us would get any sleep and I have to be at the station before the sun comes up in the morning."

He followed her to the living room and sat with her on the sofa. She watched as he laid the canvas against the wall right next to him and then turned to her.

"What did you purchase tonight?" she asked.

"Baby, we'll get to that in a second. I wanted to talk to you before I left to go home."

Zora heard the seriousness in his tone and

wondered if something was wrong.

"Is everything alright?" she asked concerned.

Micah sensed he needed to reassure her that it was. His mother was right when she said he could be overly dramatic.

"Yes baby, everything is wonderful."

He leaned over and gave her a reassuring kiss.

"Everything is fine. I want you to know that I had a great time tonight celebrating you. Thank you for inviting me. It was nice to meet so many of your friends and to see how the art world embraces you. There were some pretty famous people there tonight."

Zora snuggled closer to Micah, laying her head on his shoulder and closing her eyes, taking in the moment to just be close to him.

"Thank you for coming out to support me. Your presence meant everything to me," she said.

"Zora, you mean everything to me. I have to tell you, I never thought I'd be where I am today. After Karen's passing, I figured I would be alone for a long time because I only wanted to focus on Kaia. I thought by doing that I had to put my own needs and wants aside and that included a relationship where I would fall in love."

Micah reached down and lifted Zora's chin until she opened her eyes and he was looking directly into them.

"I love you Zora Michaels. I have not been this happy in a very long time and it's important that I you know you complete me. Thank you for once again filling my life with love and I now realize it was our destiny to meet when we did. I believe if we had met earlier than when we did, neither of us would have been ready. Fate had a hand in our meeting that day outside and I've never looked back. Only forward into a life with you and Kaia."

Zora was touched by Micah's confession of just what she meant to him.

"I love you too Micah."

"Do you realized we've known each other only a few months and I feel like I've known you my entire life. I'm thankful that I've been given a second chance at love and I don't take it for granted. I don't want to miss this chance I have to begin anew. I know it's soon and I don't want to scare you away, but I love you and I want to marry you. I want you to be my wife."

Zora stiffened, not out of fear or reservation, but because she, like Micah, never thought she could love another man as much as she loved Isaac, but here she was, with more love in her heart for this man than she ever thought possible. Nothing was happening to soon as far as she was concerned including his desire to make her his wife.

She knew without a doubt that Isaac was smiling down on her, happy that she didn't give up on living because he had died. He would not want her to be alone for the rest of her life and as much as he knew she wanted children, he would want her to find her new Mr. Right and make a life with him. She has finally done that and she wasn't going to pass up the chance to have another shot at the forever kind of love she had dreamed about.

"Micah, I love you too baby, more than I could ever tell you and yes, I'll marry you. I would love to be your wife. Now that I've found the kind of happiness I once had, I know that tomorrow is not promised and we have to live each day to the fullest. I'm ready to do that with you and Kaia."

They kissed to seal the commitment they were making to get married. Micah reached into the lapel pocket of his tuxedo and withdrew a black satin sack tied with a white satin bow and opened it pulling out a custom cut, diamond platinum engagement ring. He reached out, removed the ring from its bed and placed it on Zora's finger. He then kissed first her finger and then her lips, sealing their love.

Micah suddenly remembered that he had one additional surprise for her. He reached for the painting that was covered in paper. Before he opened it, he wanted her to know the purpose behind it.

"Zora, as I said, I believe in fate and destiny and I believe you and I were meant to be in this place, right now together. I will forever love and miss Karen and I know that you feel the same way about Isaac. I never want them to be just sad memories for us. I want us to embrace who they were and what they meant to us. I want to be sure that wherever we go and whatever we do in life, neither of them are ever forgotten. I have Kaia as a reminder of Karen and I want you to have something special as well."

He handed her the painting and watched as she opened it. He spoke as she did.

"Wherever we are, we will always carry Isaac with us as well."

Zora couldn't stop the tears from flowing when she realized Micah had purchased the painting of Isaac in his uniform. She was speechless.

"I bought this for you tonight because we will find the perfect place to hang it in our home and we'll always tell our children who he was and what he meant to you because without him, we would not be together. It was a sad occasion, his passing, but I'm thankful that together in the afterlife, he and Karen had a hand in us finding our love. Our forever kind of love."

Zora stared at the painting and after leaning it carefully back against the wall, she through her arms around Micah's neck. Nothing could have ever prepared her for the man who had confessed his love for her, asked her to marry him and then made sure she never forgot about the love she once shared and how their love is made stronger because of the love they once shared for others before each other. Each at one time thought that love only happened once and now they knew everlasting love happens a second time around.

"I love you so much," she said before moving in close for the kind of kiss she needed and just before she took his lips in a searing kiss, she watched as his lips formed to say he loved her.

Micah drew her into his arms and Zora, throwing caution to the wind that her grandmother would walk in and catch them, she moved to straddle his lap, placed her arms even tighter around his neck and kissed him with every bit of passion she could gather up. She was ready for her life to begin anew.

Epilogue
Fourteen months later

"Zora, baby do you need me to come rub your feet again? I was going to make you some lunch before I go into my office to get some work done."

Micah knew her feet were aching and swelled. It seemed that his leg and foot massages eased some of the pain.

"No, I'm fine. I'm just laying here in the bed, feeling like a whale on the beach I'm so fat. For now my feet are fine. Thanks for rubbing them earlier."

Micah entered the bedroom before going down to the kitchen.

"You are not a whale on the beach and you are not fat, baby, you're pregnant. You are what pregnant women are supposed to look like."

Zora loved her husband. They had been married for over a year and she still loved him as much today as she did the day they had gotten married, two months exactly from the day he had proposed.

Soon after, she discovered she was pregnant

with their child and they were over the moon with elation.

"Thank you honey."

"Now how about some lunch," he said trying to coerce her.

"No, I'm not hungry. I could use a bottle of water."

"Water coming right up," Micah said hurrying off.

He was happier than he ever thought he would be again. He was thankful to his parents who had come to take Kaia to a birthday party of one of the children of a family from church. Zora was so close to her due date that Micah didn't want to leave her side. He tried not to show how nervous he was after what he experienced with Karen, but every now and then it showed. Today, he would get as much work done from his home office as he could until his mother came by later to sit with Zora so that he could then go into the studio. She was due any day to give birth to their son. Kaia was especially happy, telling everyone that she was having a baby brother soon and she couldn't wait to meet him.

"Babe, I brought you two bottles because you drink water so fast, I want to be sure you had plenty. Your grandmother and my mother will be back soon and until they get here, I'll be downstairs in my office."

After getting married, Zora had sold her house and they moved into Micah's because it had more room and because he lived on the end in his cul-de-sac, he was able to add to their current house to accommodate an art studio.

Zora was thankful when they were finally able to talk her grandmother into moving with them to Boston. Micah was more convincing than she was, especially after he told her about the baby and how much they would love to have her around the kids.

Micah entered the bedroom and had not noticed the stunned look on Zora's face because he was busy moving about the room and talking.

"Honey?"

"Yes baby," Micah answered as he turned to look at her.

"I think my water broke."

Micah's heart stopped beating and he couldn't move.

Zora saw all movement in Micah stop.

"Micah did you hear me? My water broke and I think we need to get to the hospital."

Adrenaline started to flow and Micah went into super hero mode.

"Okay, I'm going to get you some clean clothes." He started walking about the room, gathering up a new change of clothes for her and helped her get into them.

"The baby's bag is already by the front door," he said nervously.

After Zora was dressed, Micah helped her get to the car.

"Are you okay? We have time right?" Micah said fearfully.

"Yes we have plenty of time. My water broke, but the contractions are still pretty light. We still need to hurry. I don't want any mistakes."

Micah turned red when she said that and knew what was running through his head.

"Don't you start worrying. I'm fine, Micah," she said reassuring him. She had no doubt he was reliving Karen's pregnancy and day of delivery.

Micah didn't answer her and that made her nervous.

Zora stopped at the car.

"Look at me," she said.

She saw worry when he turned to look at her.

"I'm fine so no worries, okay?"

Micah took a moment to compose himself and smiled so that he didn't upset her with his concern.

"Yes, no worries. Everybody is fine," he said rubbing her stomach.

After he got her in the truck, he drove towards the hospital while at the same time using the hands-free device to call his parents. When his dad picked up, Micah told him of the situation.

"Dad, I'm on the way to the hospital. Zora's water broke."

Micah heard his dad informing his mother. They were still at the party so they still had Kaia with them.

"Son, we're going to take Kaia to her other

grandparents and we'll meet you at the hospital. Where is Zora's grandmother? Is she with you?"

"No, she went with a few seniors to a play."

"We'll call her and stop to pick her up. I'm sure she'll want to be there to. Promise me you won't worry and trust that everything is going to be okay," his father said, trying to calm him even more.

"You guys drive careful and yes, I know everything is okay," Micah said, trying to sound reassuring.

"I will son. Call me with an update as soon as you hear something if we are not at the hospital when things progress."

"I will."

Micah disconnected the call just as they pulled up into the emergency entrance to the hospital. He alerted a staff person that he needed a wheelchair because his wife was in labor. A few nurses standing outside went into action. This was it, Micah thought. He said a silent prayer as he waited for them to wheel her in.

**

Zora had been in the hospital in labor for three hours and the doctor had finally said it was time to deliver their son. This was the day that Zora had longed for and she couldn't wait to meet her son. She had finally found the happiness she had longed for and now with the addition of the new baby, she had the family she always wanted. She had a loving husband, a beautiful little girl and very soon a bouncing baby boy.

Micah had gone to give his family the news that they were about to deliver the baby and he came back in the room as they were prepping her for the delivery. He looked at his wife and said thank you to anyone listening. He knew that today would be a defining moment in his life. He had been at this point before and things didn't turn out well.

After he was all suited up in his hospital gear, he joined Zora at the head of the bed. He held on to her and encouraged her to push all the while telling her how much he loved her and how grateful he was for her. Finally he looked down and watched as the doctor pulled his screaming son out.

"You have a beautiful, healthy baby boy. Micah if you'll cut the cord here, the nurse will take him, clean him up and tell you how much he weighs."

"Thank you doctor," Micah said happily.

Micah cut the cord and gave his wife a kiss of thank you. He could see tears of joy in her eyes which mirrored his.

"We'll just clean Zora up here and while we do that, why don't you go over and say hello to your son."

Micah went over and watched his son as they cleaned him up and weighed him.

"Zora, our son weighs eight pounds eight ounces and as you can hear, he has some pretty strong lungs."

He smiled as his son shouted to the world that

he was here.

"Thank you. I love you."

Micah looked over at his wife.

"I love you too."

Later in her private room, Zora held her son, amazed at how much she was already in love with her little bundle of joy. They named him Elijah Aaron Prentiss and he slept comfortably in her arms. She didn't want to put him down after waiting years to finally give birth to a child.

She looked up as the door opened and in came Micah, his parents, her grandmother and Kaia. Micah was holding tight to Kaia because he knew if he let her go, she would run and jump on the bed.

"Hi Kaia. You want to see your baby brother?" Zora asked.

Kaia shook her head yes and her long ponytails bounced up and down. Micah picked her up and placed her on the bed with Zora and the baby. He looked at the sight before him of his family and knew that with the kind of love they shared, this was only the beginning.

*Get a glimpse into the next installment of the
Amorous Occupations series with this excerpt from
"The Bookkeeper"*

Karen Jacobs walked into her office to get information on her latest assignment. She'd just returned from a much needed vacation and was eager to get back to work. She had been working for the FBI for seven years and she was about to get her first undercover assignment.

"Welcome back Ms. Jacobs," one of the office assistants said as she passed by.

"Thanks Tanya. I'm happy to be back."

"Did you have a nice vacation?"

She'd had a blast on vacation. She was an adventurists so she had done everything from sky diving, to rock climbing to deep sea diving and she loved every minute of it.

"I had a great time. I was actually supposed to have another week off, but duty calls."

"Well it's good to see you back. Mr. Jackson is in and he's waiting for you. You can go right in."

"Thanks Tanya."

Karen walked into her boss's office where he and two other agents were waiting to brief her on her assignment.

"Karen, good to have you back," Mr. Jackson said. The others in the room said welcome back as well.

"Thanks. It's great to be back."

"Why don't you take a seat and we'll brief you on what we have."

Taking her seat, she opened up the folder that had been placed in front of her. Shocked was the first thing that came to mind when she opened it and saw the face of Thomas Atwater. He was the owner of a major financial investment firm in the Raleigh, North Carolina area. He was also the man she'd walked away from ten years earlier because he had chosen work over his life with her.

Being a workaholic herself, she now understood his commitment to his work and now felt like she had been naïve and selfish back then. She had been a woman in love and he was a man on the rise in the business world who didn't have time for her. She had issued him an ultimatum and she'd lost. She looked up from the folder into the faces of the men around the room. They knew everything about her and knew her connection to the man in the picture.

"What's this?" she asked, with great surprise.

She watched as everyone around the table looked to each other, but avoided eye contact with her.

"This, Karen, is your assignment."

She looked from one man to the other wondering if this were some type of joke.

"You're not serious are you?" she inquired searching their faces.

"Karen, we are very serious about this case. We've received some very reliable information that there are some unsavory financial dealings going on at Atwater Industries. It appears that Mr. Atwater has been involved in some illegal dealings and we need you to get in and check things out. We're setting you up as a temporary bookkeeper at his firm. The last Mr. Atwater knew about you, you were an accountant so this should work out well with getting you in the door. He has no idea what you've been doing since he last saw you so your identity as an agent is secure. His current bookkeeper is about to go out on maternity leave and this is the perfect opportunity to get you in under the radar."

To say she was shocked would be an understatement and she had no doubt they could all see the reservation on her face. For starters, she knew Thomas and knew he wouldn't be dealing in anything illegal and she that with this scheme, they were reaching. Their plan sounded simple and though it may seem easy to them, she had a feeling it would not get past Thomas at all. He was too smart to think that after all of this time, she was willing to be a bookkeeper for him and it didn't matter what her background was. With the history they had, she couldn't imagine justifying getting a job at his firm.

"He won't fall for this," she said.

"We know he wouldn't fall for the fact that you just happened to be coming in for a temporary position as a bookkeeper knowing that at that time when you last spoke, you were an accountant for a major firm. He wouldn't understand why you haven't progressed much further in your career. We're setting up a background for you that includes, working in finance for a major corporation in Seattle and that you're coming back to the Raleigh area because you were tired of living on the west coast. You never did sell your parents' home after your mother passed away so it was easy making a transition for you to be back in the area, moving back into the house that meant so much to you."

She shook her head, letting them know that she didn't think that all of this was going to be possible.

"You really believe he'll fall for that? So what am I supposed to do, just walk into his company and apply for a job as a bookkeeper? Even with my history in accounting, I can't see just casually strolling into the company of a man I walked away from years ago and asking for a job."

She sat tight-lipped as her boss continued.

"We know, again from a very reliable source, where Mr. Atwater will be having lunch Monday afternoon. We want you to casually stroll into the restaurant, not his company, and happen upon him. You'll strike up a conversation as if you've forgiven him for the way things ended between you two. His lunch date will conveniently not show up and you'll sit down to join him until his guest arrives, like I stated, who won't actually show. Try to start a conversation about what he's up to these days and push for it to lead in the direction of him telling you about his bookkeeper leaving his company to have a baby soon, leaving him in a pinch to find a replacement. This is what you've been trained to do and I have faith you can pull this off without a problem."

Karen started to see it playing out in her head and realized it just might work. Her director was right, she was trained for this.

"Now, Karen, the current bookkeeper is one of our sources. She claims that there are some tricky things going on with the money. There are lots of meetings behind closed doors and one day, she was looking at the books and realized she had never seen one of them before. It contained information about major deposits into an account she wasn't familiar with. She then discovered she had been looking at the wrong book and not the one she should have been looking at. She went out to lunch and when she returned, that wrong book had been mysteriously replaced with the correct book. Someone has switched them while she was out. She asked Mr. Atwater about it and he brushed it off as if he didn't know what she was talking about. He quickly changed the conversation and went about his day. She mentioned what she saw to her best friend's husband who is a police detective and from there, the information was passed on to us. Our initial investigation led us to several off shore bank accounts in Mr. Atwater's name that contained funds that amount to much more than his company could make in a year's time."

Karen started to understand better now. They wanted her to find out what kind of on the side business Thomas was involved in and if it were anything illegal.

"I'm picturing how to play this out now," she said, feeling more confident.

Her boss smiled.

"I knew you would Karen. You are our brightest agent and if anyone could pull this off, it's you. When he mentions the pregnant bookkeeper, lead in with the fact that you're back in the area and you had not yet taken on any new jobs as an accountant. Since the past is water under the bridge, you could help each other out by having you fill in for the bookkeeper until she returns. That way, you can make a little money while getting acclimated back to the area."

Karen reassured them she was on top of it and would to take the file back to her office and prepare for her move back to the Raleigh area where she'll work closely with the branch of the FBI located in that area.

After the briefing, she headed to her office where she closed the door behind her and opened the folder again studying its contents. She stared into the face of the one man she was never able to forget. He was the man who could play her body like a sweet guitar, picking every string that turned her into putty in his hands. She closed her eyes and remembered the many nights of passion they shared, knowing she had never met a man since who made her feel the way he had.

She looked down into the face of the most handsome man she'd ever laid eyes on and wondered if she were going to be able to resist him long enough to get her job done. She hoped so because her boss was counting on her. She could no longer be the Karen who was still madly in love with Thomas Atwater. She now had to be Karen Jacobs, the FBI agent who would find out about the illegal dealings and if she had to, she would make sure he was prosecuted to the fullest extent of the law.

Karen closed the file and walked to the window to look out. She knew she would do her job, but at the same time, she couldn't wrap her mind around the fact that the Thomas she knew would be involved in anything criminal. Either way, she would get to the truth and put her game face on to prepare.

Get your copy of The Bookkeeper, the second book in the Amorous Occupations series, available in September 2013 in paperback and e-Pub.

Other romance novels available by
Cheryl Barton:

Bachelor Series

Bachelor Not For Sale
Duron & Taija's story

A Designed Affair
Loren & Mike's story

Perfect Combination
Tyrone & Victoria's story

ABOUT THE AUTHOR

Cheryl Barton lives in Maryland and in her down time she enjoys reading mystery, espionage and crime stories, writing, spending time with her family, crossword puzzles, line dancing and most of all, enjoying Maryland steamed crabs. You can connect with her Twitter @authorcherylbarton, Instragram @authorcherylbarton and on Facebook at Author Cheryl Barton. You can find information on upcoming novels by visiting her website at www.cherylbarton.net.